Return to
Tatanka Crossing

The war has been over for three years but only now is Charlie Jefferson returning home.

If he has changed during his absence, so too have the inhabitants of the Wyoming valley he left behind. Neighbourliness has been replaced by greed and hostility; the cluster of buildings around Sam Flint's trading post has developed into a small township where gun-carrying saddle-tramps congregate; and a man called Brent Deacon is forging an empire at the expense of the original settlers.

Choosing to interfere on behalf of Lars Svensson, who is accused of murder, brings Charlie into conflict with the dangerous Deacon, but the reasons for their animosity are much more personal.

Return to Tatanka Crossing

Will DuRey

A Black Horse Western

ROBERT HALE · LONDON

ISBN 978-0-7090-9839-3

Robert Hale Limited
Clerkenwell House
Clerkenwell Green
London EC1R 0HT

www.halebooks.com

Typeset by
Derek Doyle & Associates, Shaw Heath
Printed and bound in Great Britain by
CPI Antony Rowe, Chippenham and Eastbourne

CHAPTER ONE

If Charlie Jefferson jumped to the conclusion that the rider across the river was Ruth Prescott, it wasn't to be unexpected. She'd been predominant in his thoughts for days, ever since he'd begun the trek north from Texas; ever since he'd decided that he'd delayed his return long enough. Ruth was one of his reasons for coming home; probably the major reason. When he'd ridden off to war she'd vowed to wait for him, told him she'd watch for his return every day, and now, in the first instant of realization that the pinto rider on the far bank was a girl, his homecoming hopes appeared to be fulfilled.

Even when the first little doubts entered his mind he refused to believe that the girl wasn't Ruth. The fact that he was yet several miles from Tatanka Crossing and that it was a further two-hour ride beyond that to the Prescott ranch only vaguely indicated to him the likelihood that the person under his inspection wasn't Ruth. And the blonde hair that had fallen to her shoulders when she'd removed the flat-crowned, black hat was fairer, less yellow than he remembered, and worn in a ponytail. Ruth had always avoided that style, adopting other ways to wear her hair which made her appear more ladylike than cowgirl. But he had been away almost six years. His habits had changed in that time, it was natural to assume that Ruth's had, too.

It wasn't until she removed the buckskin waistcoat she wore, turned it inside out and replaced it so that the black underside showed, that Charlie realized the girl was too slim to be Ruth. Not only that, she was too young. This girl was no older than Ruth had been when he'd gone off to war, probably younger, and the emotion that had momentarily filled him now dissipated as quickly as it had grown. Disappointed though he was by the realization that the rider wasn't Ruth, he still watched, intrigued by her behaviour.

She had come into view upriver from where he'd stopped to refresh himself and Smoke, his grey gelding, riding below the ridge on the tree-lined slope, which fell sharply at first, then more gently to the lush riverbank. She'd pulled up the black-and-white pinto at the edge of a faint trail leading to a much-used crossing point, and had looked back in the direction of Tatanka Crossing, turning the horse in circles, keeping him active as though anticipating company that would excite horse and rider into action. Then she'd begun with her wardrobe, first removing the black hat, revealing the blonde hair that told Charlie the rider was a girl. This she hung by its cord around the saddle horn. Then she changed around the waistcoat which she was wearing over her off-white shirt, and finally she tucked her hair back inside an old, grey, soft hat, which she pulled out of a saddle-bag. Two minutes later they came.

The first rider topped the far ridge, cast a glance behind but, without any noticeable restraint of his mount's headlong flight, began the run down to the river. He was slim, a youthful rider dressed in black trousers and a white shirt partly covered by a black leather waistcoat.

On his head he wore a grey hat. His similarity to the girl who had been under Charlie's scrutiny did not end there. He, too, rode a black-and-white pinto and the difference of its markings from those of the animal the girl rode were not immediately clear. The pinto seemed eager to complete its downhill charge, its ears back and tail flying, but barely had it started on its way than the rider pulled it to a walk, waved a hand in acknowledgement of the girl's presence, then turned the horse towards a particularly dense clump of elderberry bushes, many of which were scattered along the incline on that far bank. Within seconds horse and rider had disappeared from sight behind the foliage.

Adopting a position which would ensure maximum speed from the mount she rode, the girl put heel to horse. Low in the saddle she rode, her body stretched forward, her head close to the horse's neck. The black-and-white pinto raced down the far embankment at almost reckless speed. Obviously accustomed to this stretch of the trail, horse and rider crossed the watercourse without falter, fearless of what might lie beneath the surface. On reaching Charlie's side of the river they galloped up the slope towards the timber line of willows and cottonwoods.

No sooner had the pinto strided clear of the water, however, than across the river, topping the high bank at the same point where the first rider had come into view, came four more riders. They rode upright in the saddle, more cautious as their mounts plunged over the escarpment, doubtful of the pluck of the beasts as they tackled the sharp drop that began the descent. The earth subsided slightly beneath their weight and they slid and juddered their way, past the bush where the first rider remained hidden, down to the easier slope and the firm ground of the riverbank. A shout went up from one of the four as the fast moving pinto was spotted, then gunshots, two, fired without any hope of hitting their quarry because the distance between was too great for a revolver, but the noise served to announce their presence, a signal of their intention which drew a backcast look from the girl in front.

The four splashed through the shallow, quick-running stream, less wary than they might have been of underwater hazards because their quarry had already crossed without mishap, and when they gained the other bank the two whose pistols had already been discharged, fired again. One of the others yelled for the shooters to save their ammunition, the black and white pinto was already among the trees and lost from sight. Soon, they too had urged their mounts up the slope and were ducking and weaving among the trees before disappearing over the escarpment beyond.

Thirty yards downstream, Charlie Jefferson witnessed the brief flurry of activity, his presence unknown to any of those who had ridden by. They had been too intent upon their own role in the drama to pay attention to anything on the periphery. The girl had been intent on drawing the attention of those behind and reaching the cover of the trees without mishap. Accordingly, she had adopted a riding position which maintained focus on what lay ahead, twisting away from Charlie, facing upstream, except when glancing back at the sound of the pursuers' gunfire. And the pursuers looked neither to right nor left as they crossed the water. Already it was clear that their mounts were more ponderous than the pinto, and keeping them on course was task enough for the riders, who were careless of anything that was not in their direct line of pursuit.

Charlie had remained motionless when the four had appeared. He'd watched as, in less certain fashion, they'd followed the pinto's trail down to and across the river and he'd studied the determination on the faces of the pursuers as they'd splashed through the stream, firing useless bullets in the direction of the lone rider. The two who had fired their weapons were typical ranch hands; their clothes grubby, their faces dark due to a mixture of weather, stubble and trail dirt, and with a meanness in their look that denoted a tendency to violence. One wore a red shirt above his denim pants and the other a blue one. The third man, the one who had given the order to stop firing, was tall, clean shaven and riding a chestnut travelling horse that was bigger and had a deeper chest than the rangy cow ponies of his *compadres*. He wore a cord jacket and a light-coloured hat which, although not new, had managed to retain its original shape. He rode with an air of authority, clearly in charge of the little group.

The last member of the group was the youngest and wore a badge of office attached to his leather waistcoat. The shots, when they were fired, seemed to surprise him, as if heralding a turn of events that hadn't been part of the plan. For a moment he seemed to pull on the reins, unprepared to continue the pursuit, but by that time they were plunging into the stream and the cold spray from the horse in front seemed to give fresh impetus to his own mount. The order to cease fire after the second volley didn't remove the uneasy expression from his face but he stayed with the others as they tackled the incline up to the trees.

At the sound of gunfire the rider who had taken refuge behind the elderberry bush emerged into Charlie's view. He watched the pursuit until all the riders were out of sight, then, unaware of Charlie Jefferson, he turned his horse upstream and rode away.

Charlie Jefferson and Smoke were weary travellers. Their journey north from Texas had taken several weeks. Behind them were the dry, dusty lands of the Indian

Territories and Kansas. Now, so close to their destination, Charlie was reluctant to ask more of Smoke. He'd broken camp at sunup, knowing that this was the last day of their journey. Already that morning they'd covered several miles, stopping only to refresh themselves at this familiar stream he knew as the Feather Waters because their destination lay less than an hour away. He'd allowed Smoke to dip his head in the water while he wiped away the accumulated dust and sweat from his own face and neck with a cold, soaked neckerchief. But curiosity now had the better of him. He tightened the cinch, climbed into the saddle and turned the gelding towards the ridge they'd recently descended. He urged Smoke on in the wake of the other riders, his interest aroused. The incident was too close to home to be ignored.

Charlie brought Smoke to a halt when they got to the crest of the ridge over which the riders had disappeared. Only a short while ago he'd breasted this ridge from the opposite direction and had been gladdened by the sight of the cool stream valley which lay below, knowing that this was the beginning of the fertile north land fed by water from many sources among the Rockies. Now, facing the opposite direction, it seemed that the heat and discomfort he'd endured for the previous three days assailed him again. He raised his hat with his left hand and wiped his brow with the same shirtsleeved arm.

Before him was a panorama of incalculable extent. The land stretched west and east without any significant feature to mark its limit, and ahead, the far horizon was the blurred, purple smudge of the southern hills. Three days earlier he had crossed those hills. What distance he had travelled since he couldn't rightly say but it had been hard and dusty land and the view he now had reminded him of its inhospitality. Below, and beyond the immediate maze of giant boulders, lay a giant bowl of scrubby grass. From his vantage point it resembled a huge lake that had drained away and left behind a hostile, sun-baked terrain.

Until reaching the stream, dust had, to Charlie, been a throat burning, eye-watering irritant. Now it was an indicator of the horsemen's location. It rose, hovered and dissipated, marking their twisting progress among the randomly strewn boulders on the plain below. Down there it was easy for a rider to set a trail that would obscure them from the view of anyone trailing, winding in and out between twenty-feet-high boulders that at ground level were not only obstacles to sight but demanded caution by those in pursuit. Up high, Charlie was able to see the dust trail of the horsemen, and, from time to time, catch a brief glimpse of the men themselves as they followed a haphazard trail on a south-westerly course. All thought of following them was chased from his mind. Smoke was in no condition to try to reduce their lead. What did surprise Charlie, however, was the fact that he couldn't see any dust raised by the girl. Of course one horse wouldn't raise as much as four, but it still seemed strange not to see any at all. In addition, there had been no glimpses of that rider along the open stretches, as there had been of the others.

Charlie sat on the ridge for a moment longer watching the dust until he realized it was beginning to settle in one spot. Momentarily he wondered if the pursuers had caught their quarry but the answer to that question became manifest when the pinto and its rider emerged from between two boulders almost directly below him.

At the foot of the ridge they halted and, presenting only a back view to Charlie, the girl undertook in reverse the changes to waistcoat and hat she'd earlier performed on the other bank of the river. Charlie rode Smoke among the cottonwoods when the girl began to make her way back to the ridgeline. She, too, kept to the timber covering to ensure she wasn't visible on the skyline to her distant pursuers. For a moment she paused to check their location. Satisfied that she'd given them the slip, she turned the pinto to the descent to the Feather Waters, waded through, then climbed the rise to the far ridge, sparing a glance at the elderberry bush that had acted as cover for the real object of the posse's pursuit. Assured that he was long gone, she continued on the trail towards Tatanka Crossing.

Charlie Jefferson waited until she'd cleared the far ridge before following. He had no expectation of catching the girl because he wasn't prepared to push Smoke to anything more than a walk. In any case, it seemed certain that their paths would soon cross. If her destination was Tatanka Crossing it was not far from his own. He'd recognize her again, that was certain, but something in his consciousness told him that he wouldn't have to go looking for her, that this incident wasn't yet done with him.

As it happened, they met sooner than Charlie anticipated. Not far from Tatanka Crossing, along the escarpment that hovers above the Tatanka river by which Sam Flint had established his trading post, he came across her examining the pinto's off foreleg. Charlie Jefferson was almost upon her before she heard his approach. Startled by the stealthy arrival, the girl ceased her examination and took a position by the pinto's head, holding the bridle and gathering the reins in case the stranger came to cause trouble. As Charlie got closer her initial cautious expression was replaced by a smile.

'Hi,' she said.

'Everything OK?' Charlie asked.

'Fine. Just fine. A cut on her hoof got infected a couple

12

of weeks ago but she's fully recovered now.'

'Need to take care of her. Don't want to be riding her too fast.'

Wariness returned to the girl's expression. She climbed into the saddle aware of a knowing edge to his tone. She cast a look back along the trail they'd both used and for a moment was troubled by the possibility that he'd witnessed the events by the far stream. But he was casting an eye over her horse, looking pleased with what he saw. She spoke as they began to make their way down the embankment towards the town, putting a little laughter in her voice, hoping to twist the conversation in another direction. 'She can go fast. Do you want a race?'

Charlie grinned. It had been a long time since anyone had offered him such a challenge. Not since the gatherings in this valley, before he went to war. Racing had been a popular event in those far-off days and he'd been one of the most successful riders. He shook his head. 'You'd have the advantage of me. Smoke here can hardly raise a canter, at present.'

The girl eyed the big grey horse with what, to Charlie, seemed a very critical eye. 'You've ridden him hard,' she said.

'Not hard. Just far. He needs a rest.'

'Well, offer still stands. Whenever you're ready.' She smiled mischievously and added, 'But you won't win.'

Charlie noted the blue of her eyes and the dash of freckles across her nose and upper cheeks. 'You're pretty sure of yourself, young lady,' he said. 'Smoke has a fair turn of speed.'

'Ah yes,' she replied, 'but Collie here,' she patted the pinto's neck, 'was bred on the Svensson ranch.'

'One of Taub Svensson's horses! Then you're a lucky girl. Nobody knows horses better than Taub.'

'You never could beat one of his horses, could you?'

'That's not true. And how would you know? Hey, do you know who I am?'

'Of course I know you, Charlie Jefferson.' She let the smile on her face fade and adopted an expression of effrontery. 'Do you think I'd offer to race against any dusty saddle tramp? What kind of girl do you think I am?' By now they'd reached the first buildings of Tatanka Crossing. She turned her horse as though to ride off, but before she did she threw another smile at him over her shoulder, and a few more words. 'I'll tell Pa what you said. Come a-visiting, Charlie Jefferson. We'll be happy to see you anytime.' Then she rode off up the street, leaving Charlie in front of the building that he had helped to build when only nine years old: the original trading post.

CHAPTER TWO

As he watched the girl ride along the street, dismount and hitch the pinto to a rail, Charlie analysed her parting words and came up with her name. She was Taub Svensson's daughter. Jenny, he recalled, who had been little more than a baby when the original families had first settled in this valley, and barely a teenager when he'd headed east to join the Union army. His silent deliberation also came up with a name for the rider for whom she'd acted as decoy; her twin brother, Lars. The similarity of form and face had been remarkable when they were children and Charlie recalled how alike the two riders had been at the far side of the river, not only in the garb they wore and the horses on which they were mounted, but also their physique and mannerism. It had been difficult to distinguish one from the other. It didn't explain why Jenny had undertaken such a risk, but, whatever the cause, his knowledge of the Svensson family prompted his favour. She was on the boardwalk now, looking back to where he still sat astride Smoke. Charlie sensed that she was smiling at him. He touched the brim of his hat in acknowledgement, then she was gone.

It had not been his intention to ride through Tatanka Crossing. The trail to his father's ranch ran along the embankment where Jenny Svensson had been examining the pinto's leg. But for that encounter, Charlie would have stayed on the trail home. He wasn't sure why he had ridden down to the township with her; perhaps hoping to glean the reason for her behaviour at the river; perhaps amused by the invitation to race; or perhaps for no reason at all except that riding beside her had seemed the most natural thing to do. Now that he was here he realized how much had changed since his departure.

Fifteen years earlier, when he'd first stood on this spot alongside his parents, brother and the members of the other eight families that his father had led from Missouri, there had been nothing here. The long valley stretched before them – high, wooded slopes, acres of fertile pasture land and a slim, constant flowing stream which wended north-easterly to a junction with the North Platte. There was no indication that any man had ever passed this way before. There were no buildings or cattle herds, no cultivation of the land or bridges across the water. Nothing here but the land itself, good land, land as fertile for harvesting crops as it was lush for rearing cattle. They saw the land and wanted it. It was land on which to settle and leave their mark, land to develop and leave as a legacy for their descendants.

So those original settlers explored the valley and agreed boundaries that would divide it into eight portions, each having its share of timber, grazing land and access to water. As Charlie's father, Dagg, had been their leader, he was allowed first choice. He selected the section at the southern end of the valley. The other families, the Prescotts, Svenssons, Dunstons, Kelloggs, Humboldts, Johnsons and Castleways drew lots and spread northward to build their properties and establish their stock.

Sam Flint arrived alone in the valley. His wife, along

16

with Ezra Prescott's wife and eldest daughter had been buried along the way. Their three graves on a knoll over-looked the Republican, their death attributed to a harvest of some unrecognized berries. Subsequently, with no other family to provide for, Sam had chosen to forgo a rancher's life, choosing instead to act as trader, haulier and blacksmith for the families. His trading post was log-built, long and low and situated near a shallow crossing point of the Tatanka. Around it, over the passing years, more buildings had been erected and the small gathering became known as Tatanka Crossing.

The winters were hard, snow coming in a swift fury that was capable of trapping the animals in deep drifts. The first two winters caught the new ranchers unprepared, much of their stock freezing to death on the open range before it could be rounded up and brought close to the homestead. The losses of the second winter were enough to discourage the Johnsons and Castleways who, when the sun heated the land again, travelled south to the Oregon Trail to join up with the first wagon train heading to California. Their land was absorbed, Dagg Jefferson expanding over most of Bill Johnson's share and Ezra Prescott becoming the main beneficiary from Seb Castleway's departure.

For those who remained in the valley their lives were industrious but, in the main, content. The cattle herds increased and, after the disaster of the first two winters, their vegetable crops yielded sufficient to satisfy each family. Fulfilling his role as agent for the families, Sam Flint negoti-ated the sale of steers and excess vegetables with the military at Fort Laramie. Cattle were driven there twice a year.

In the early years, without nearby professional people, all matters were resolved within the valley. The families took care of themselves; tended their own ailments, settled their own disputes, buried their own dead and taught their offspring the things they needed to know to help the family prosper. Those who had come after them, if they stayed, were obliged to follow the same creed. From time to time an army patrol would put in an appearance, its arrival welcome but always edged with caution lest it wasn't just the bearer of news from beyond the valley but the herald of tribal hostilities against the white man. No more than once a year they'd receive a less welcome visitor – a travelling preacher seeking donations from those who had little but the land on which they lived, cajoling them with threats of fire and brimstone and, on more than one occasion, attempting to seduce the wives and daughters while the men folk were abroad, tending the stock. Neither of the two who left the valley puffed up with self-satisfaction made it to their next congregation. But there was no law west of the Missouri at that time; no sheriff to apprehend those who had 'jerked to Jesus' the errant preachers; no judge to try anyone who might have been apprehended.

Newcomers to the valley were welcome as long as they were prepared to work for one of the existing ranchers. No-one else was permitted to run cattle on the range. Some came and stayed, finding employment on one of the spreads. Others came, worked a summer round-up then drifted on again. Only one man tried to buck the rule. His name was Grice; he tried running cattle on the Jefferson range. He'd been chased away, his beasts confiscated and when he returned with a bunch of armed men he encountered a united force of valley families. All the invaders were buried where they fell. The message was clear: This valley was spoken for. There was no room for anyone else.

Charlie was fifteen at that time and the settlers were eventually beginning to show some prosperity. The herds were larger, outbuildings more numerous and hired hands on the increase. Drifters, having heard of the valley from tales passed on by wagon scouts and soldiers, rode in, but only those with the intention of finding work on one or other of the ranches ever stayed. Sam Flint's trading post was no more than that. He'd sell a jug of whiskey to anyone who could pay for it but his establishment wasn't a saloon bar where men could gather to play cards or dally with dance-hall girls. Without those attractions there was nothing to persuade drifters to stay.

Now, as Charlie gazed along the extended street, he noted all the high-fronted buildings that had been erected in his absence. There were signs, too; Sheriff's Office; Barber; Milner; Bank; Saloon. At the top end of the street there were new buildings under construction and the street was busy with people, men and women, going about their daily affairs. Out of habit, he'd stopped outside the original trading post. As a youth he'd spent many hours inside; sometimes stacking goods for Sam Flint; sometimes listening to travellers' tales. Soldiers, wagon train scouts and adventurers all had yarns to tell, but Charlie's favourite visitors were the mountain men fresh down from the hills, enjoying their first contact of the year with civilization as they made their way to St Louis, prepared to swap a tall story and a fine beaver pelt for a jug of whiskey.

It wasn't until he'd taken his weight from Smoke's back that he noticed there had had also been changes to this building. A new high-front had been added and a sign board that proclaimed Deacon's Mercantile in large red letters. He was still wondering why Sam Flint's name wasn't on the board when he passed through the door into the well-remembered store house. Little natural light got into the store but as Charlie's heeled boots clattered on the hard, wooden floor, he knew that the internal layout had not changed. There were still sections for hardware, dry goods, canned goods, fancy goods and clothing. What had changed was the atmosphere.

The old trading post had been a vibrant centre for the people of the valley. Even when there were no customers inside it seemed busy with expectancy, as though prepared and eager to assist the next person who entered. Now the darkness within, which had once been a token of welcome and security, hung about the place like an unfriendly bear. The man in the apron behind the far counter viewed Charlie with suspicion.

'Where's Sam Flint?' Charlie asked.

'Never heard of him,' the man replied.

The answer surprised Charlie. He remembered the name on the board outside. 'You Deacon?'

'No. I just work here.'

Charlie looked around. No one else was in the store. 'Quiet,' he observed.

'Can I get you anything?'

Charlie shook his head. 'Just came in to see Sam Flint. If he's not here I'll go.' Slowly he turned and headed back to the street. As he reached the door, four horsemen passed by. One wore a red shirt, one a blue shirt, another rode a fine chestnut and the fourth had a star attached to his leather waistcoat. The front rider, the cowboy in the red shirt, was pointing ahead, exhorting his companions to follow his lead. Charlie guessed that Jenny Svensson's pinto had been seen and that the little posse was eager to make an arrest. He hurried down the street in their wake.

By the time he caught up with them a small crowd had gathered around the rail where the pinto was hitched. Charlie could hear Jenny, her voice resonant with indignation and, he suspected, a little fear. 'You've got no right to search my saddle-bags,' she shouted. 'I haven't broken any laws.'

'Harbouring a fugitive is against the law,' observed red shirt as he stepped forward to grab the saddle-bags slung across the pinto's back. Jenny got herself between the man and her horse, a grim look on her face, defying him to take the matter further. 'Your brother is a killer.'

'He is not,' denied Jenny.

'Sure is,' sneered the man, 'and you and your family are hiding him. You'll go to prison too if we prove you're aiding him.' He made to move forward again and Jenny pushed her hands against his chest to keep him away from Collie. The man reached forward, grabbed both ends of her shirt collar and heaved her aside, into the arms of the tall man who had been riding the chestnut. Jenny struggled to break free of the man's grip but he was too strong for her.

From those gathered around arose a murmur of protest. The man in the red shirt stared at each of those who appeared to be the most angered by his action. No-one raised any other objection.

'Now let's see what there is in here.' He was undoing the fastening of the bag when Charlie Jefferson pushed through the crowd, grabbed his shoulder and spun him around.

'Men don't treat ladies like that where I come from,' he said.

Startled by the rough interruption, the man in the red shirt glowered. 'And where do you come from?' he asked.

'Here,' said Charlie. His right fist came round in a wide arc, delivering a haymaker which landed flush on the other man's jaw. Red shirt went backwards, arms flying high, legs splaying wide and he landed with a loud thud on the dry, dusty street.

With a yell the man in the blue shirt launched himself at Charlie. Instantly, he threw a right that was blocked by Charlie's left. In return, he received a short-arm uppercut to the midriff from Charlie's right which doubled him over. Although he saw the next punch coming, there was nothing he could do to stop it. It was another right-arm punch which caught him on the left side of his face, below the ear, jerking his head to the right, causing his whole body to turn as he fell, leaving him unconscious, on his face, in the street.

The big man, the one who had grabbed Jenny when she'd been manhandled away from Collie, pushed her aside and thought briefly of intervening in the affair. His hand went to the butt of the ivory-grip pistol that hung in a holster on his right hip. If his draw was hampered by indecision, it probably saved his life. By the time his hand had encircled the butt and begun to pull upwards he discovered that Charlie's gun was already in his hand.

'You'd better take your hand away from that pistol,' Charlie told him, 'and let Miss Svensson mount her horse.' Jenny came forward but threw an angry glare at the man. Charlie waited until she was in the saddle. 'You,' he said, indicating the young man wearing the star, 'are you a lawman?'

'Deputy sheriff,' he declared.

'What reason do you have to search this lady's belongings?'

'Her brother is wanted for murder. We followed him on that pinto,' he declared. 'She must have met him with a fresh horse so that he could escape.'

'You're wrong,' Charlie told him. 'Miss Svensson was out riding with me. There were plenty of people around when we arrived in town together. Make your enquiries; someone will vouch for us.' He turned his attention to the big man. 'If I hear of anyone molesting Miss Svensson in the future, you'll be the first one I come looking for and you'll get the chance to try your luck with that pistol.'

There was silence among the crowd that had gathered

22

as he began to back away up the street towards Smoke. Jenny Svensson kept pace with him and paused outside Deacon's Mercantile while Charlie mounted the grey. Then they rode out of town together.

No words were exchanged until they had gained the high ground above the town. 'You'd better give me that grey hat,' Charlie said, indicating the saddle-bag where he'd seen her stow it after eluding the posse. She gasped in surprise, having convinced herself earlier that he was unaware of her part in her brother's escape. 'That's a dangerous game you are playing,' he told her.

'They could never catch Collie, and what could they do if they did?' she asked, defensively. 'I'm not the one they've accused of murder.'

'They weren't trying to catch you, Jenny. They were trying to kill you. And Collie can put her foot in a rabbit hole as easily as any other horse. You're gambling with your life. I'm sure Lars doesn't want you to do that.'

'He needs help,' she said. 'He's accused of killing a man.' Hurriedly, she added, 'He didn't do it.' She sniffed, trying to hide her emotion, not only overcome by thoughts of her brother's predicament but also affected by the incident in town.

They'd reached the fork in the trail that led off to the Jefferson ranch and although he was anxious to know more of the accusation against her brother, he was also aware that this wasn't the time to be asking questions of the girl. Jenny needed to compose herself. As neither of them expected her to be accosted again by the four man posse, they prepared to part. 'I'll take up that invitation to visit,' he told her.

A smile tugged at the edges of her mouth. 'Good.'

'Is tomorrow too soon?'

'Come to dinner,' she said. 'Ma and Pa will be pleased to see you.'

23

CHAPTER THREE

Dagg Jefferson spotted him when he was nothing more than a slow moving silhouette high on the ridge. Took him, at first, to be one of their ranch hands, or a neighbour, or just some drifter searching for employment. As he got closer and Dagg failed to identify the rider, he studied him more closely. The horse was coming on at nothing better than a slow walk but even the distance between them couldn't hide the purposeful manner of the rider's approach.

Dagg shielded his eyes against the sun and watched. Something in the way the man's shoulders moved jarred at his memory. The shoulders were different now, broader and deeper, filled out like the rest of the torso which was upright from the saddle. He put down the axe he'd been using, propped it against the door post and opened the ranch house door. He spoke without averting his gaze from the approaching rider, fearful, perhaps, that if he stopped watching he would disappear and never return again.

'Mary,' he said, 'come outside.' His voice was low and gentle, as unlike his normal manner as it was possible to be. Yet, for his wife, that very timidity conveyed urgency and commanded immediate obedience. His words struck

her as a portent of an exceptional event, as an alarm call
to prepare for the unexpected.

She came into the sunshine drying her hands on the
long calico pinafore she wore over her grey cotton dress.
Following her husband's gaze she shielded her eyes with
her right hand to watch the rider. 'Who is it?' she asked.
'Tommy Humboldt?'

Dagg Jefferson looked at his wife and slowly shook his
head. 'It's Charlie.' He felt her hand on his arm, pressing
hard, using him for support. He heard the catch in her
throat as she tried to repeat the name and he saw the
wetness in her eyes as she tried, unsuccessfully, to control
her emotion. By the time Charlie reached the house his
mother had abandoned her attempt to hold back her
tears. She wept against her son's chest while his father
gripped his hand and studied his face, trying to fathom
the character of this man who had left them when little
more than a determined youth.

The need for food, its preparation and consumption,
eventually brought a semblance of normality to the
Jefferson homestead. While his mother busied herself with
pots and pans Charlie took Smoke to the stable, unsaddled him, gave him a drink then rubbed him down with
handfuls of clean straw. With his mount tended, Charlie
set to washing away the trail dust that had settled on him.
His mother's home-made soap didn't produce much
lather or have a particularly pleasant smell but it cleaned
the skin just as well as the fancy store-bought products
he'd had occasion to use on his travels. He was drying
himself on a piece of rough towel cloth when his brother
rode in.

'Charlie?'

Charlie flung aside the towel and reached for his shirt.
'Your very own brother, John. How are you?'

25

'I'm fine. Just fine. How about you?' As he asked the question John looked pointedly at the long slash of puckered skin that scarred the left side of Charlie's body, high up, near the shoulder.

Charlie put on his shirt. 'I got that instead of a medal,' he said, giving a twist to his lips that was meant to pass as a smile. 'Come on, wash up. There's a meal ready and I haven't eaten home cooked food for six years.'

A lot of questions were fired at Charlie as they gathered around the table, but he was paying too much attention to the food to give any detailed answers. His mother had spread a clean cloth over the sturdy table and brought out the best dishes but no one paid them any attention. Charlie's concentration was entirely for what had been put on the plates and the other three scarcely took their eyes off him, still not certain that the man at the table was their son or brother.

'We've been expecting you since the war ended,' said Mary Jefferson.

'Things didn't work out that way,' he said, glancing up at her face, reluctant to talk about his life for the past two years. 'I wrote.'

'Wrote,' said Dagg. 'Seven letters in six years. You call that writing?'

'It wasn't easy, Pa. During the war we were either marching or fighting. There wasn't much I could put in a letter.'

Dagg put down his fork in a manner that suggested he had arguments to offer but Charlie's grey eyes held his in a steady, determined gaze. The look told him that there were things in his son's life which weren't for discussion at the family table. In any event, his wife spoke first. Her words were intended to pour oil on troubled water. 'It doesn't matter about the letters. The war is over and we have Charlie home all in one piece.'

'Almost,' said John.

Charlie cast an angry glance at his brother.

'What's that supposed to mean?' Dagg asked.

'It means I got hit in the shoulder by a lump of shrapnel. I'm fine now. Doesn't bother me at all. There's a scar. That's all.'

Silence filled the room for several seconds. Eventually, Dagg spoke. 'When did that happen, son?'

'Last few weeks of the war. I was in a field hospital when Lee surrendered.' He looked around the table. It was clear from the inquisitive expression on each face that they expected him to supply more details about the action in which he'd been injured, but he wasn't about to comply. 'But those days are gone. Much more important for you to tell me what's been happening here. Seems like the settlement's grown some while I've been away.'

'Did you ride through Tatanka Crossing on the way here?' Dagg asked.

'I did.'

'Then people know you are home.'

Charlie thought his father's voice held a note of caution. He glanced around the table. Each member of his family was concentrating on the food on their plate. 'People know,' he said. Then a quick smile touched his face. 'All the people in town were strangers to me. All except one. I met young Jenny Svensson along the ridge.'

'Jenny's a nice girl,' said Mary Jefferson. 'I'm surprised you recognized her. She could only have been twelve or thirteen when you went away.'

'I didn't recognize her. She recognized me. Offered to race against me.'

Dagg chuckled. 'Was she on a pinto?'

'Yes.'

'Don't be drawn in, Charlie. That horse can run faster

than anything I've ever seen and' no one rides it better than Jenny. In fact, that girl has a gift with horses. Her father reckons she knows more than him and you won't have forgotten his reputation.'

'Certainly not.'

Dagg nodded in the direction of Charlie's brother. 'I keep telling John he should marry the girl. We'd then have the best cattle and the best horses in the valley.'

It was clear from John's response that this was a subject, even if only aired half-seriously, of which he was weary. 'Pa! She's just a kid.'

'She's old enough. Wouldn't you say so, Charlie?'

'She looked well past being a kid to me.'

'See, John,' said his father, 'and if you don't make a move for her someone else will. Someone else will get the benefit of that expertise. Taub says she tends all his sick and injured stock.'

'Pa!' said his wife. 'That's no reason for him to marry Jenny Svensson.'

'Sure it is—' he began but the sound of approaching horses interrupted his argument.

John crossed to the window to see who was visiting. 'It's Deacon,' he said. 'He's got three men with him.'

Dagg Jefferson stood up and went outside. As he passed the rifle rack on the wall near the door he paused a moment but continued out through the door without selecting any weapon.

'Is that the Deacon who owns the mercantile?' Charlie asked his mother.

She nodded.

'Owns the Last Dollar saloon and runs the bank,' added John who was lifting down a rifle from the wall rack, 'and he wants to ruin Pa.' He followed Dagg out on to the veranda.

28

Charlie cast a glance at his mother seeking some sort of explanation for his brother's remark, but Mary Jefferson simply got to her feet and went to join her husband and elder son. Charlie had removed his gunbelt when he sat down to eat. Side-arms had been a rare sight in the valley before he left to fight in the war. In the Jefferson household, at least, it seemed like a fashion that still hadn't caught on. His father and brother worked around the ranch unarmed. For Charlie, however, travelling from town to town since the end of the war, a Colt on his thigh had been a prerequisite. He collected his gunbelt from the chair on which he'd left it and strapped it around his waist. Easing the gun in its holster a couple of times, he stepped outside.

The four men hadn't dismounted. They sat astride their horses in a line, space between each of them. The man doing the talking held the leftmost position. He had pushed his black Stetson to the crown of his head, displaying his full forehead and front hairline, looking casual, as though he'd called to invite the family to a church picnic. He had a neat, small moustache and wore a blue, heavy cotton shirt with a narrow strip of black ribbon tied in a bow at his throat. He had big teeth and dark eyes and he smiled as he talked.

'The bank's calling in its loan, Mr Jefferson. You've got 'til the end of the month.'

'The bank knows it'll get its money. I'll repay what I borrowed when the cattle get sold at Fort Laramie. That's the way we've always done it.'

'Well there's a problem with that this time.'

'Problem?'

'They can no longer take your cattle at Fort Laramie.'

'Why not? They've bought their beef from this valley for fifteen years.'

'Times change, Mr Jefferson. The cattle dealers have all moved nearer the railhead.'

'But we sell direct to the army. Sam Flint had an arrangement with them.'

'Yeah. But Sam Flint's no longer here. Seems the new commander at Laramie has swept aside that old arrangement. They've got someone who can supply their full quota.' Apart from the buzzing of the flies, which irritated the horses, a heavy silence hung between the group on the veranda and those mounted in front of it. Deacon spoke again. 'So your debt needs to be cleared at the bank before the end of the month or you lose this ranch.'

'You're not touching anything on this range, Deacon,' said Dagg Jefferson. 'This is my land and I'm keeping it.'

'Only until the end of the month if your debt isn't cleared. That right, Sheriff?'

The man to the right of Deacon was red faced with a long, drooping moustache. His high hat was dimpled at the crown and crumpled at the edges. He was a tall man. Slim and relaxed, his hands rested on his saddle horn. 'That's what the bank's lawyer says, Mr Jefferson. If you don't fulfil your debt then your land is forfeit. That's why I've come along, to let you know it's legal.'

Charlie Jefferson stepped forward, away from the ranch house door, out of the shadows. 'You got some document to show how this is legal, Sheriff?'

The sheriff turned his attention to Charlie. 'No, no document.'

'Then what are you doing here? Have you come to uphold the law or to act as the bank's mouthpiece?'

The sheriff shifted in the saddle, his eyes narrowed; his right hand moved from the saddle horn to rest on his right thigh. 'I don't know who you are, young man, but someone should have taught you to have a bit more respect for authority.'

'My name's Charlie Jefferson and you are the second lawman I've met today who seems to think that his presence makes legal the actions of other people.'

The sheriff stiffened in the saddle. 'Are you the rannie who drew iron on my posse?'

'I wouldn't be proud about calling them your posse, Sheriff. I stopped four men from assaulting a young girl. Any man who picks a fight with a girl is no man at all.'

'They were doing their duty.'

'Their duty was to make sure of their facts before laying accusations against citizens. Like I told your deputy, Miss Svensson was riding with me this afternoon and unless you can prove otherwise, the matter ends there. Now, you're on Jefferson land where you've got no jurisdiction. Get off. Like my pa said, no one is taking anything from it. Not ever.'

'Well, well,' said Deacon. His grin widened. 'Charlie Jefferson. I've heard a lot about you. I daresay my name's familiar to you, too. Brent Deacon.'

'No,' said Charlie. 'Never heard of you.' Deacon's surprise showed and Charlie was sure it was genuine. 'But whoever you are, get off our land now and don't come back.'

The grin returned to Deacon's face. 'We're going but I can't promise we won't be back. I'll give your regards to my wife.' With those words he turned his horse's head and rode away with the other three close on his heels.

CHAPTER FOUR

'Somebody want to tell me what's going on around here?' They were back in the house, wearing expressions of anxiety, nervousness or anger; perhaps all three. Dagg was rolling a quirly, John was inspecting the Winchester he'd taken from the wall rack and Mary Jefferson was fussing about the table as though needing her husband's help before deciding what to do next, eventually settling for refilling cups from the coffee pot. 'Why do you owe that man money?' Charlie asked.

'Because he bought Pa's debt,' declared John.

His brother's angry words didn't add much to Charlie's knowledge. He looked to his father for clarification. 'I borrowed money from the Cattlemen's Bank in Laramie to buy out Cyrus Kellogg. I didn't want him selling his land to Ezra Prescott who had already bought Eli's place. Ezra Prescott owning half the valley didn't seem right to me.'

'Slow down, Pa. I've got a lot to catch up with. Cyrus Kellogg and Eli Dunston have left the valley?'

Dagg hesitated, catching his wife's fluttering movements, knowing that on this day she didn't want any talk of turmoil, didn't want anything to cast a pall over her son's return home. But he looked at Charlie, studied the intensity of his expression and knew that he was a man who faced his problems head on. There was nothing to gain by withholding details of the situation for another day. Besides, John was so full of anger that the facts were sure to tumble from his mouth before they were all an hour older.

'Even though we had a regular source of income from the sale of beef to the army,' he began, 'money was scarce during the war. The army was paying bottom dollar for our beef, which was only just enough to keep our heads above water. With the small herds that Eli and Cyrus were running they were barely surviving year by year. They would have accepted the offer they received at the end of the war but the buying consortium wanted the whole valley. The rest of us weren't interested in selling. We were confident enough that with the war over the price of beef would rise and we'd be OK. Besides, we'd found this valley and developed it. We had no reason to uproot and move elsewhere. We weren't going to put in all the hard work so that someone else could benefit. Even Ezra Prescott agreed with me at that time.'

'Why wouldn't he?'

Dagg looked at his son with a stern expression, held his tongue for a moment, giving Charlie the impression that what was to follow would wound him. 'Ezra never got over Amos leaving with you. He blamed you for taking him away and he blamed me for allowing you to go. When news came that his boy had been killed his anger knew no bounds.'

'I wrote to him, Pa. It might not have been much of a letter but I wanted him to know he could be proud of his son.'

'Charlie, I got to tell you, Ezra's a bitter man. Some say he's sworn vengeance against you. It's probably nothing more than angry words but, in truth, he hasn't spoken to me since we heard the news. I went to visit him and he chased me off with his shotgun. If Ruth hadn't been there he might well have pulled the trigger.'

At the mention of Ruth, Charlie pictured her face. Even though it was a long ride, he'd had it in mind to borrow one of his father's horses and visit the Prescott ranch once the meal was over. But the recent visitors had brought about a change of mind. He couldn't leave his family until he'd learned every detail of the current situation. To divert his thoughts from Ruth he asked about Eli Dunston and Cyrus Kellogg, seeking an explanation for their departure from the valley.

'Soon after the war ended,' his father continued, 'Eli Dunston had an accident. Fell off his horse fording the river and drowned. His wife sold out to Ezra Prescott and moved away. Shortly after that a couple of incidents unsettled Cyrus Kellogg. First there was a fire in his stables. He managed to get the horses out but the building was razed. And a few days later one of his night riders was killed in an unexplained cattle stampede. Cyrus came to tell me that Ezra had made him an offer for his land. It was a poor offer but Cyrus was on the verge of accepting. Ezra's animosity towards us was already hardened by this time and it didn't seem right to let him dominate the valley, so I offered Cyrus more for his spread.'

Dagg paused to light up the quirly he'd rolled while talking. 'Of course,' he went on, 'I didn't have enough money of my own for the deal. Sam Flint introduced me to a man called Balfour at the Laramie bank, who had arranged loans for other cattlemen. He understood the advantage of increased grazing land by the river. We worked out repayments for a five-year loan which weren't going to cripple me as long as our cattle sales remained constant. I used the deeds of this place as collateral for the loan.'

34

Charlie scratched his jaw. 'You haven't been able to keep up the repayments?'

'Everything was fine until Sam Flint was killed.'

'Sam's dead?'

'Yes. Ma would have written to let you know but we didn't know where to send a letter.' Charlie shuffled on his seat. He didn't need reminding that the prolonged absence had been his own choice. 'Another accident,' his father continued. 'Young Jenny came across him when running one of her father's mares. His neck was broken. As far as anyone could figure, it happened at night. Looked like he'd ridden into a low-hanging branch.'

'Sam! Riding at night? Sounds unlikely, doesn't it?'

Dagg shrugged his shoulders, confirming that such a thing sounded odd to him, too. 'Nobody could figure out what he was up to. There is only this place and the Svensson ranch close enough to the settlement for anyone to come visiting at night and, other than the Spring and harvest gatherings, Sam had never come a-visiting before. Neither Taub nor I had any business with him that would have brought him out at night.'

'Sam Flint was a good man,' said Mary Jefferson, her tone indicating an opinion that life hadn't been fair to him. Charlie guessed she was thinking about the loss of his wife so early in their marriage, but her words prompted no response from anyone else in the room, the silence testament enough to confirm their agreement with the sentiment. Charlie had liked Sam Flint. He'd numbered renewing their acquaintance among the benefits of returning to Tatanka Crossing.

'Wasn't cold in his grave before Brent Deacon took over the trading post,' said Charlie's father.

'Who is Brent Deacon?' asked Charlie.

'Nobody knows much about him. Arrived in Tatanka

35

Crossing shortly after the war ended, then hung around for a few weeks without any apparent desire to find work. When Sam died he announced he'd had some experience of running a merchant enterprise back in Pennsylvania and that he was keen to settle down here.'

'Sounds like an ideal candidate.'

'Yeah,' said Dagg, 'but things changed rapidly after that. Whereas Sam had been unselfish in his efforts on behalf of the cattlemen in the valley, Brent Deacon proved to be a businessman with an eye for his own profit. Don't get me wrong; I'm not opposed to a man prospering by means of his own endeavour, and Deacon's schemes always had initial appeal, but they ended up making him rich and bringing disruption to the valley.'

'I rarely go into town,' said Mary Jefferson. 'It's become the haunt of a lot of unpleasant people.'

Her husband nodded his agreement. He drew in the smoke from his hand-rolled cigarette, then slowly exhaled it before speaking. 'A logging company set up a camp on the slopes across the river, bringing with it loggers, mill workers and teamsters. Just a handful at first, but the enterprise grew. Then deposits of copper were discovered in the rocks a little way west of here, enough of it to grab the interest of some Cincinnati developers who have been mining it for three years. Neither activity interferes directly with our cattle business but the effect on the settlement has been enormous.

'Of course, with all the extra men in the valley it wasn't long before it was no longer suitable to use the back room at the trading post as a meeting place. There was drunkenness, fights broke out, men cussing and blaspheming when the womenfolk were on the other side of the room buying provisions. It just couldn't go on.

'So Deacon proposed building a new hotel, leaving the

trading post free for its original purpose. The hotel would not only cater for the social needs of the current work-force but would also be a welcome resting place as more and more people travelled west. The Last Dollar was built further down the street. Perhaps you saw it when you rode through town. Deacon calls it a hotel but that's a mighty polite name for what goes on there. There's a saloon bar and gambling tables on the ground floor, bedrooms above.'

He snorted derisively. 'The gamblers came first, looking to take from the men the money they had earned labouring in the mine or logging camp and even herding cows in the valley. Then there were girls housed in the upstairs rooms to take whatever money was left over. When men meet, a combination of whiskey, money and girls leads to only one thing; fighting. The men who now come to Tatanka Crossing all seem to come prepared for trouble. None of them seeking work. All of them happy enough to hang around the saloon, guns strapped to their thighs, waiting for something to happen.'

Quizzically, he looked at the weapon tied to his son's leg, as though seeing it for the first time but nonetheless aware that wearing it was commonplace for Charlie.

His father's look was noted by Charlie, but he gave no apology for wearing the gun. To him, towns like the one Tatanka Crossing had become were not rare; on his travels he'd seen many like it. They had sprung up all over the West, wherever necessity caused men to settle. In such towns, carrying a gun was essential for survival.

'Has there been trouble?' he asked.

'A lot of fistfights. A few shootings. Two deaths.'

'Which brought a law officer to town?'

'Brought the sheriff, brought a doctor and an under-taker. Brought a lawyer, too. According to Brent Deacon these are the trappings of civilization. Professional people without whom the town of Tatanka Crossing has little chance of developing.'

'But you're not sure you want it to develop?'

'Managed well enough without those people for fifteen years. Now your Ma and the other womenfolk from the ranches are afraid to go into the settlement. Seldom get into the store to see what's new. Drunks hang about the streets, careless of speech and behaviour. When supplies are needed it's become a job for one of the ranch hands.'

Charlie sipped his coffee. John's earlier words still nagged in his mind: the accusation that Brent Deacon was trying to ruin his father. Coupled with that thought was the memory of the scene that had recently been played out on their front porch. His dislike of Brent Deacon had been instant. His manner, his sarcastic smile and mocking tone had immediately impressed upon Charlie that this was not a man to be trusted. Moreover, there had been the hint of something personal between them; a threat; a conflict; a mortal duel. In Charlie's opinion, Brent Deacon wasn't just untrustworthy, he was a harbinger of violence. However, nothing his father had so far said had shed any light on why or by what means Brent Deacon meant to destroy his stake in the valley. He put down his cup and spoke to his father. 'I'm still curious about why you owe Brent Deacon money.'

'Because he wants to control Tatanka Crossing and the whole valley,' interjected John. 'Not content with the money he was making from the mercantile and saloon, he proposed opening a bank.'

Dagg spoke placidly, as though sensing a need to suppress John's anger. 'It seemed like a good idea at the time. There's always been a deal of risk attached to transporting money between here and Fort Laramie, so when Deacon proposed opening a bank in Tatanka Crossing we all agreed to support it and transfer our money away from the Cattlemen's Bank in Laramie.' Dagg paused, rubbed his jaw with a big hand as though unsure of the words he needed to continue his story. However, his gaze was fixed on his son's face and Charlie knew there was more to come. 'I wasn't particularly worried when I got a letter from Balfour at the Laramie bank informing me that in addition to transferring my savings to the Tatanka Crossing bank, Brent Deacon had also adopted my loan.'

'Why did he do that? Did you speak to him about it?'

'Of course I did. Told me it was sound policy for the bank to have full knowledge of their customer's finances. Makes it easier for the bank to assess future requirements, he told me. He made it sound like a sensible argument.'

'But now he's threatening to throw us off our land for non-payment of the debt.' John couldn't disguise his anger.

'You can't pay?'

Charlie had directed the question at his father but it was John who responded with vehemence. 'I've told you, Deacon is trying to ruin us.'

'Pa?'

'John's right. While he was alive, Sam Flint continued to be blacksmith and carter as well as trader and agent for the cattlemen in the valley. It was thanks to Sam that we in the valley were able to concentrate on the business of raising cattle. If something needed doing that we couldn't do for ourselves then Sam would do it or arrange for it to be done. He had our total trust. Although he didn't have the necessary papers he was as good as a lawyer for us, organizing deals and financial arrangements with the relevant authorities in Laramie.

'But Deacon has never had time for the cattlemen. He's

cosy with the men who see themselves as civic leaders of the town. Men like McFadden from the logging camp and Brewster who's in charge at the mine. Then there's Sheriff Simms and Ben Carter. He's a lawyer. They all seem to spend time at Deacon's hotel, congregating in his private quarters, drinking special whiskey and smoking fat cigars.'

'Then there's the other sort that hang around him,' John added. 'Like those two who came here with Deacon and the sheriff. The worthless sort who look like they're just hanging around waiting for a fight to start.'

Dagg took a last draw on the thin cigarette before speaking again. 'Whenever we cattlemen wanted the use of his wagons he'd claim they'd been contracted out to the mine or timber people, often leaving it to the last minute to inform us, putting our own enterprise in jeopardy. He'd delay trips to Laramie for much wanted goods or claim he had been contracted to haul a full load for the timber or mining people and we'd have to hold off for another month. Because of his delays we didn't get our usual quota of cattle sold to the army in the spring, and now it seems they've cut us out altogether. That income was needed to pay off this year's instalment on the loan. You heard what the sheriff said; non-payment means we forfeit this ranch.'

Charlie growled. 'It won't come to that.' He picked up his cup and took a mouthful of coffee. He smiled at his mother. 'Good,' he told her.

She returned his smile, acknowledging his appreciation. 'It should be, the price we have to pay for it now.'

'All prices at the mercantile have increased,' said her husband. 'Everything is almost double what it was when Sam was in charge. Deacon claims that profit from liquor sales used to subsidize the sale of other merchandise. Since closing the bar-room he's raised the price of all other commodities. In protest, Tommy Humboldt, Taub and I amalgamated to get our own supplies from Laramie.'

John spoke up. 'That hasn't worked out too well either, has it, Pa?'

Dagg Jefferson shook his head. 'Could have been worse, I suppose.'

'What happened?' Charlie asked.

'Five men attacked Tommy Humboldt on his way back from Laramie a couple of weeks ago. He took a slug in the leg. He'll be fine, but his driver was killed. The wagon was overturned and the goods dumped in the river.'

'Did Tommy recognize the men?'

Dagg shook his head. 'They kept their faces covered. Tommy told us some saddle tramps were watching him carefully when he was loading up at Laramie. He reckons they were the ones that did it.'

'Did they get much?'

'No, nothing. For some reason they skedaddled when the wagon went over. Tommy thought that perhaps they were scared off by someone coming along the trail, but no one showed up for almost an hour after the attack. Tommy came close to bleeding to death before he was found.'

'Most likely,' said John, 'they'd been paid to stop the goods getting through and assumed that that had been accomplished when the wagon overturned.'

Silently, Charlie agreed with his brother but another thought had pushed its way into his head that needed airing. 'Lars Svensson is accused of killing a man. Is this the incident?'

'You know about that?'

'There was a bit of trouble in town. Jenny told me her brother is wanted for murder.'

'No. This is not the incident.'

Dagg Jefferson lowered his head reluctant, it seemed to

Charlie, to impart any further details. 'Who is he accused of killing?' Charlie asked. 'Feelings were running high among certain individuals in town.'

'Jed Prescott.'

'Ruth's brother?'

'A couple of witnesses claim to have seen an argument between Lars and Jed. I don't believe Lars killed anyone. He isn't a violent boy.'

'What does Lars say?'

'He hasn't said anything. His accusers shot at him on sight and he had to flee. Now there's a reward on his head. One thousand dollars, dead or alive.'

'That's a lot of money. Ezra wants him bad.'

'Ezra didn't put up the money. Brent Deacon did.'

'This all part of being a civic leader like you talked about, or were Jed and him close friends?'

'Not friends, Charlie. Family. Last year Brent Deacon married Ruth Prescott.'

CHAPTER FIVE

Three men gathered in the small room which acted as Brent Deacon's office in the Last Dollar. Deacon occupied the armed seat he used when working at the desk. This night, however, because he wasn't poring over stock figures or correspondence since documentation of the current discussion was unnecessary, he had moved the seat to a position that provided more comfort; it enabled him to stretch out his long legs and ease those muscles that had been worked that afternoon by his increasingly rare need to climb on a horse. It also had the effect of putting at ease the other people in the room, allowing them to believe they were his equals, his confidants, his trusted advisers.

Sheriff Simms had settled himself on one of the high-backed chairs that were stationed along the opposite wall, indulging in the whiskey and slim cigar proffered earlier by Brent Deacon. Had they not been the best available in Tatanka Crossing, the sheriff would not have been such a regular visitor to Deacon's office, but, despite the unease he often felt when in the company of his host, he was not a man to deprive himself of any available pleasure.

The third man was the tall rider who had led the four-man posse. He had a long face, with a long, straight nose above a long, thin-lipped mouth. His eyes were so narrow

43

that they seemed barely capable of fulfilling their function but it was by watching those eyes that a man might judge his mood, for only the small folds of skin at the corners recorded any change of expression on his bland face. Never, though, was that expression one of happiness; satisfaction, perhaps, when he'd belittled, wounded or maimed someone else, but usually it was one of indifference to the discomfort of others, or superiority because men knew that he wasn't afraid to pull the trigger of his gun to achieve his own goal. His name was Gus Tarleton and, unlike Sheriff Simms, he hadn't availed himself of a seat. Instead, he stood to the right of the door, his left leg bent so that the sole of his foot was pressed against the wall behind. He smoked his own tobacco, a black cigarette from which the smoke rose fine and blue as opposed to the billowing grey puffs with which the lawman was filling the room.

'The Svensson kid got away again!' Deacon spoke to Tarleton, his words neither a question nor a criticism, but the other knew he needed to offer an explanation.

'We had him trapped at his parents' ranch. We could have taken him there but you said to do the job out on the trail. Away from witnesses.'

'Yes, yes.' Deacon spoke quietly, as though the fact that Lars Svensson had slipped through his fingers was a temporary matter, a nuisance in comparison to a more troublesome problem. 'And you're sure the girl was at the ranch when the Svensson kid left?'

'She was there when he arrived and nobody left the ranch while we were watching.'

'And you reckon they switched horses somewhere.'

'Among the boulders at the other side of the Feather Waters. He'd led us there in a big loop, which gave her plenty of time to get ahead of us by using the direct trail.'

'Seems like they knew you were watching the place,' said Deacon.

'Perhaps. Or perhaps they were just taking precautions.'

'You lost him in the same place last time,' Simms said before filling his mouth again with whiskey. Any criticism was obscured by his obvious satisfaction at Tarleton's failure.

'Next time,' Tarleton said, 'I'll stay at the ranch when he leaves and follow the girl. If she wants to get involved she'll have to take the consequences.'

Brent Deacon studied the cold expression on Gus Tarleton's face and wondered what manner of consequence he intended to visit upon the girl. As long as there were no repercussions for him he didn't really care, but communities like Tatanka Crossing tended to have little tolerance for men who mistreated womenfolk; a fact already demonstrated by Charlie Jefferson.

As though his thought of Charlie Jefferson had been spoken aloud, Gus Tarleton said, 'And no matter what that saddle tramp says, she wasn't riding with him all afternoon.' His right hand dropped to the Colt tied to his thigh. He lifted it partly clear of its bull-hide holster then allowed it to slip back into place. Charlie Jefferson had held a gun on him and publicly threatened him, insults which he couldn't allow to pass unpunished. He'd seen Charlie's quickness with a gun but that didn't deter him from wanting revenge; he'd never been averse to setting an ambush for someone who was faster than himself. Again he touched his gun, a clear indication to Deacon that he awaited his instruction to use it.

Brent Deacon noted Tarleton's eagerness to take care of Charlie Jefferson, but for the moment killing Charlie was not in his plans. He had been aware of the expectation in the valley that when Charlie returned home from the war he would marry Ruth Prescott, but a union of the Prescott and Jefferson families would have forged a hold on the valley which would have been difficult to breach. His plans would be more easily achieved if there was a rift between the families so, when he'd learned of Ezra Prescott's festering resentment following the battlefield death of his youngest son, he had taken every opportunity to rub salt into his wounds.

When, finally, Ezra openly declared that he would never allow his daughter to marry Charlie Jefferson, Brent Deacon had taken her himself. Now he wanted to increase the humiliation on Charlie; now he wanted to prove that he was the power force in the valley by taking away the Jefferson home. Forcing the Jefferson family from the valley would be a major step in the completion of his plan.

'Not yet,' he told Tarleton. The inkling of a scheme scratched at Deacon's imagination. There were no details yet, just the desire to use Charlie Jefferson's homecoming to add to Ezra Prescott's aggravation, perhaps use it to incite his fledgling feud into violence; spark off a range war that would encompass the whole valley. He didn't have to wait long for an opportunity to arise.

Sheriff Simms had returned to his office and Brent Deacon and Gus Tarleton had commandeered a table in the main body of the saloon. They had been there less than two minutes when two dusty cowboys shouldered their way to the bar. One of them was stocky, fair-haired and had a flat, round nose, which marked him out as Ezra Prescott's son just as clearly as the Circle P brand burned into the rump denoted a Prescott steer. Zach was Ezra's eldest child, and now his only surviving son. When the families had first arrived in the valley Zach had been fifteen years old, two years older than John Jefferson who was nearest to him in age. Zach had considered himself an adult. He worked as hard as his father and most of the other men in the valley but, to his chagrin, he was counted among the children by the other families. His opinion was never sought, nor considered when given. Consequently, he harboured a grudge against almost everyone and took it out on those who were younger. He considered himself both physically and mentally superior to the other young-sters and was happy to use his fists on anybody who didn't agree. Although he'd grown into a good stockman and rancher his character was still delineated by a surly coun-tenance and a quick temper. He was always happy to bully anyone weaker than himself.

Zach Prescott looked around the room while the barman filled two glasses from a beer keg under the counter. His eyes settled on his brother-in-law. The two men seldom socialised. Brent Deacon's manner was too haughty for them to ever rub along in comfort, and Zach had been opposed to his sister's marriage. The reason for that, however, had been purely selfish. Ruth had taken care of her father and brothers ever since her mother had died and Zach didn't want that to end. Brent Deacon, however, conducted all his business in town and he had had a large house built at the far end of the street for his new bride. When Ruth left the ranch, the domestic order she had maintained went with her.

Deacon raised a hand, beckoned Zach to his table. 'Have you heard, Zach,' he said to his brother-in-law, 'Charlie Jefferson is back.'

The news startled Zach. The recent death of his brother, Jed, had shocked his father, and the loss of a second son had brought back the bitterness of Amos's death and renewed rants against the Jefferson family. The vows of vengeance uttered by his father were lodged in

Zach's mind and now they were stirred by the cold stares of the men seated at the table. Brent Deacon and Gus Tarleton seemed to convey the message that Charlie Jefferson's return was a personal challenge to him, that it was his duty to avenge the dead Prescott brothers. Wordlessly, unsure of his next move, he walked away.

When Zach returned to the beer and companion waiting at the bar, Deacon gave his instructions to Tarleton. 'Work on Gus. Ply him with drink and persuade him you would have had his brother's killer if Charlie Jefferson hadn't interfered. Get him good and mad. Perhaps he'll get the job done for us without any blame coming our way.'

Gus Tarleton wasn't too sure that he wanted someone else to do the job; he was anticipating the satisfaction of pulling the trigger on Charlie Jefferson himself, but for the moment he was prepared to go along with Brent Deacon's instruction. After all, Deacon was paying the bills. Across the room the two men who had ridden in the posse with him, Hank Swales in the red shirt and Seth Woodlow in the blue, sat at a table with a couple of girls from the upstairs rooms. Gus signalled to them and the three crossed to the bar to engage Zach Prescott in conversation.

When Zach knew he would not return home that night, he dispatched his companion back to the ranch with the task of informing his father of every detail of Charlie Jefferson's return to Tatanka Crossing. Full of whiskey and poisoned thoughts in relation to Charlie Jefferson's part in Lars Svensson's escape from the posse, Zach allowed one of the Last Dollar's sporting girls to guide him to her first-floor bedroom where, sprawled in Dancing Annie's bed, he muttered threats and curses against Charlie Jefferson until the rotgut whiskey completely overcame his senses and he remained motionless until another day dawned.

CHAPTER SIX

The rosy colour of dawn was still spreading west across the grassland when Charlie Jefferson lit out from his father's ranch. He'd thrown his saddle over the roan mare picked out the evening before while talking with his father. Dagg, in fact, had done most of the talking, eager to tell his son of every event in the valley for the last five years. Charlie had been more reticent, speaking briefly about the last battle, the one in which Amos Prescott had been killed and he had been wounded, but he was reluctant to mention the awful scenes of carnage or the sense of injustice that filled him because his friend had died and he had survived. Nor did he give his father any indication of why it had taken him so long to return home once the war was ended. 'This and that' was the only answer he'd given when Dagg asked him what he'd done in the past two years.

This early start to the day was because of Charlie's need to be back in Tatanka Crossing when the bank opened for afternoon business. It had been agreed over supper that Charlie and his father would approach Brent Deacon, try to negotiate an agreement over the repayment of the loan. But first, despite Dagg's opposition, Charlie had set his mind on visiting Ezra Prescott; he felt he owed it to Amos to speak to his father. In addition, if there was bad blood between them, he needed Ezra to realize that though, at the moment, he considered it to be one-sided, he wasn't afraid of his threats.

The easy-paced ride to the Prescott ranch took the best part of two hours. By the time he got there the sun had climbed high and, once clear of the pines on the lower hill slopes, the heat was touching uncomfortably on his neck. He approached the gateway to the compound at an easy walk, holding his hands high and wide to show they were empty except for the leathers. Beyond the rails, several cowboys were setting about their chores, some crossing the yard from the bunkhouse to the horse corral where another couple were already stepping up into the saddles on their rangy ponies. One or two threw an unconcerned glance in Charlie's direction but his arrival caused no interruption to their routine. Not until he reached down to unhitch the leather loop that held the gate closed.

A shot rang out. A splinter of wood leapt up from the post near Charlie's hand and struck his cheek. Charlie grunted. He could feel the slow trickle of blood on his face. Instinctively, his right hand dropped towards the butt of his Colt but he remembered he'd come to heal the breach between the families, not widen it.

Ezra Prescott, squat, a head like a small boulder resting almost neckless on his shoulders, stormed across the compound from the veranda of the ranch house. He wore a small moustache, greying now like the hair at his temples. His eyes were small, hard little brown stones that glinted with anger and menace. His nose was flat and round, as Amos's had been, the only similar feature between father and son but sufficient to remind Charlie of his friend. Ezra worked the ratchet mechanism of his Winchester as he approached, making sure there was another shell loaded as he pointed the weapon at Charlie.

'There's no need for that,' said Charlie. 'I'm not here to cause trouble.' His right hand went to his cheek, scooped at the trail of blood which was beginning to drip on to his shirt.

'Jim.' Ezra Prescott's voice was sharp, like a whipcrack, issuing an order that was carried out as Charlie inspected the blood on his hand. One of the mounted men who had drifted off to Charlie's right, threw a loop over him and with a quick tug pulled it tight, trapping Charlie's right arm across his chest. Charlie yelled at the man, tried to loosen the rope by working his right arm back and forth across his body until the rope rose to his shoulders. He could hear Ezra Prescott's voice, giving orders to get him off the horse. Charlie shrugged to get the loop clear of his shoulders but kept his right arm enclosed as he did so, knowing that without it there the noose could be tightened around his neck as he tried to get it over his head. At that moment he had no reason to suppose that Ezra Prescott wouldn't finish what he'd started.

Before he got the rope clear of his upper arms, Charlie was dragged over the horse's rump and crashed to the ground. Hands grabbed him and a punch hit him low in the stomach. He tried to retaliate but was restricted by tugs on the rope whenever an opportunity to strike back presented itself. Unprepared to submit to the manhandling, Charlie used his shoulders, warding off the nearest assailants with the strength of his upper body. Then he took another punch in the gut and somebody kicked away his legs. He fell, heavily, face forward into the dirt. Slightly winded but still struggling, he was dragged to his feet. 'Hold him,' he heard Ezra Prescott command, then his struggle ended when the wooden stock of a rifle crashed against his shoulder. Charlie sprawled forward, dust filled

51

his mouth and nostrils as a boot was planted firmly on the back of his head.

Eventually, two men lifted Charlie to his knees. One removed his pistol and flung it aside, the other grabbed a handful of his hair and pulled his head back, forcing him to look into the barrel of a Winchester. Ezra Prescott's face was at the other end. 'I swore I'd kill you if you ever came on my land, Charlie Jefferson.'

'Why don't you then?' Charlie's lips were curled in anger. 'But it'll be murder, Mr Prescott, 'cos you've got no good reason for doing it. Then the law will come and hang you and we'll both be gone from the world. What good will that do anyone? It'll keep turning without us just as it's still turning without all those who died in the war. Including Amos.'

At the mention of his son's name Ezra Prescott lifted his head. 'I know you blame me for Amos going to war but you're wrong. I would have gone without Amos and he would have gone without me. No, sir, you are well wide of the mark if you think I influenced Amos. We had different reasons for going and his were a good deal more worthwhile than mine. After listening to the tales of the mountain men who came to Sam Flint's backroom I had an itch in me to travel this continent and the war gave me an opportunity to scratch. Nobody expected the war to last more than a few months and I went off because I was eighteen and wanted adventure. I don't think I even knew which side I wanted to join when I left here. I'd probably have joined the first army I came across. But it was different for Amos. He believed in the Union cause. Understood the effect it would have on the settlement and development of valleys like this if slavery was allowed to spread west. He was fighting to preserve what you were developing here, Mr Prescott. He was defending your way of life.'

In the short pause that followed Charlie pictured himself sitting across a small fire from Amos. It was their last night together. Earlier that day they'd been in a skirmish with some rebels who had attacked them with rocks and sticks because they had no ammunition for their weapons. 'Why don't they just surrender?' he'd asked.

'We're on their land,' Amos said. 'If invaders tried to take our valley wouldn't the families defend it to their last breath? That's the way it is; if you want to keep what's yours you have to fight for it until you've got nothing left to fight with.'

Ezra removed the rifle from his shoulder but his finger was still inside the trigger guard and the barrel remained pointed at Charlie.

'I needed him here,' stated Ezra. 'Needed him to work on the ranch, build it into our own little empire, not go marching off like a bugle-blowing glory boy to die in some territory on which we had no claim.'

'I guess he just saw things different to you, Mr Prescott. When you're twenty you develop your own dreams. Yours brought you here along with my own family, Amos's took him away.'

'Took him away and got him killed,' Ezra said.

Charlie was still on his knees, still held by the men he'd fought, keeping him upright while they held his arms. Blood from the splinter cut was trickling to the corner of his mouth. He spat a little of it into the dust before speaking again.

'Don't ask me why he had to be killed in our last battle before the surrender, and don't ask me why it was him and not me, Mr Prescott, 'cos I just don't have the answers. All I know is that if it had been the other way around, if Amos had been the survivor, he'd have visited my folks to tell them how it was at the end. That's why I've ridden over

53

here this morning, to tell you your son was a good soldier, a whole lot better companion and a fine man. He deserves more respect than this. He wouldn't want you trying to start a feud with people who have been your friends for years.' He spat more blood away from his lips. 'I was just fourteen when I helped build that barn behind you. Do you remember that, Mr Prescott? Do you recall when we first came to this valley? How everyone helped each other? Think of all the time my Ma spent with Ruth after your wife and eldest girl died on the trail. Ruth provided you and your sons with a fine home because of what Ma taught her.'

'I've only got one son now,' growled Ezra.

'I was sorry to hear about Jed.'

'Not sorry enough.'

'What do you mean?'

'Yesterday, you helped young Svensson escape the posse.'

'Bah! That's ridiculous.'

'Are you denying you drew a gun on the deputy.'

'All I did was chase off four men who were molesting a young girl. I would have done that no matter who the girl had been.'

'They were a posse. They wanted to question her.'

'They had a strange way of going about it. Besides, wouldn't it be more sensible to question her brother? He's the one accused of Jed's murder but my understanding is that nobody has given him the chance to answer that charge.'

'He'll answer in court.'

'A thousand dollars dead or alive! Seems to me the guilty verdict has already been delivered and that the boy will be dead long before he ever sees a courtroom.'

Ezra Prescott shifted uncomfortably, as if Charlie's

54

words were itching powder in his boots. 'There are witnesses,' he said, somewhat weakly.

'The way I heard it there were only witnesses to an earlier conversation. That doesn't make anybody guilty of anything. There have been a lot of changes while I've been away, Mr Prescott, but it still takes more than a rumour of an argument to persuade me that anyone in the Svensson family would be guilty of an act of violence. You've known Taub and his family as long as I have; what do you think?'

'People change,' Ezra said, his voice trying to retain the toughness of his initial outrage but it had clearly dissipated. Although the Winchester he held remained cocked, Ezra's finger was no longer on the trigger and it was pointed at a spot on the ground close to the gatepost. 'Let him go,' he told the men holding Charlie.

Charlie stood, rubbed the blood from his mouth, smearing it across his cheek. He walked the ten strides to where his pistol lay, picked it up and pushed into its holster. Then he climbed on to the roan mare and gathered up the leathers. 'What happened to your boys is not what anybody wanted, Mr Prescott, but there's nothing anyone can do about it. It doesn't mean you don't still have friends in the valley. My folks say they'll be pleased to see you whenever you choose to call.' He tipped his hat and began to turn the horse's head.

'My girl,' called Ezra, his voice gravelly as though wanting to maintain animosity with Charlie, 'she's married now. You stay away from her.'

'She's another man's wife. That's the end of it as far as I'm concerned.' He swung the horse, kicked its flanks and began the ride back to Tatanka Crossing.

His brother was the first person Charlie recognized when he arrived in town. John was on the boardwalk outside the bank, hat in hand, talking to a girl in pink gingham who wore a shawl around her shoulders, a bonnet on her head and carried a basket on her arm. So involved were they in their conversation that Charlie had dismounted and was standing at John's shoulder before his brother knew he was there.

In business matters and around the ranch John was a confident, often outspoken young man, but in the company of girls he was clumsy and tongue-tied. It had always been that way and now, having his brother come upon him at an intimate moment, meant that the best he could manage was a stammered introduction. The girl was Lucy Kincaid whose folk ran the eating house further down the street. While Lucy and Charlie became acquainted, John stood to one side, shuffling his feet as though nervous that one or other might say something to embarrass him.

It was immediately obvious to Charlie why his father's attempt to match his eldest son with Jenny Svensson was having no success. The looks that passed between John and Lucy made it quite clear that his partiality for her was matched by hers for him. She was a pretty girl with a cluster of freckles across her forehead and green eyes that hinted at a determined spirit. The stray strands that had escaped the tightness of her bonnet were red and Charlie thought that her appearance had all the hallmarks of a daughter of Ireland.

Eventually, when Dagg Jefferson came from the livery stable where he'd left his team and flatboard wagon, Charlie tipped his hat in parting and went with his father to the bank.

'Funny thing,' said Dagg as they headed for the door, 'when I was crossing the street I could swear I heard wedding bells.'

'Nice girl,' Charlie said.

'A cook,' said Dagg. 'Not as enticing as getting the best horse doctor west of the Missouri but a good meal is important to a rancher, too.'

Charlie laughed, but the merriment ended when they stepped inside the bank.

Brent Deacon stood at the end of the cashier's counter, beside a door that led to a private rear room. He was accompanied by the tall man from the posse, the man on whom Charlie had held a gun on at the culmination of the affray over Jenny Svensson. There were no customers in the bank, the only other person present being the teller. When he asked the Jeffersons if he could be of assistance to them, it was Brent Deacon who answered.

'I believe these gentlemen have come to see me.' He stood still, waiting for Charlie or Dagg to speak.

'In private,' said Charlie.

Brent Deacon shrugged, gave a smile similar to those he'd offered yesterday at their ranch, supercilious, telling them he held the winning hand and wouldn't relinquish it, but he opened the door beside which he stood and ushered them in. Charlie was surprised when the tall man followed them in. 'Who's this? he asked.

'I thought you two had met.' Deacon looked from one to the other, enjoying the enmity between them, aware of the stand-off that had occurred and confident that his own man had the whiphand over every other man in town. 'This is my associate, Mr Tarleton.'

'Tarleton?' repeated Charlie.

'Gus Tarleton,' said the tall man, his eyes never shifting from Charlie's face, his thumbs hooked menacingly in his cartridge belt.

'Tatanka Crossing is a long ride north from Kansas.'

'You've heard of me?'

57

'I've heard of you. Rare for you to be in a bank without your face covered.'

Gus Tarleton pushed away from the wall against which he leant, his hands hanging loose now, the right one not far from his gun handle.

'Gentlemen,' said Brent Deacon. His voice betrayed an edge of humour but he seemed content to prolong the friction between them until another occasion. 'I believe we have business to discuss.'

'I'm asking for more time,' said Dagg Jefferson. 'If the army doesn't want our steers then we need to gather up a herd and drive them to the cattle pens in Cheyenne. There are cattle dealers there. I'll be able to raise enough to cover what I owe.'

Deacon spread his hands. 'If the decision was mine alone I'd be happy to consider what you say,' he replied, 'but it isn't. We're a small bank. We haven't got the funds behind us to carry debtors. You know yourself, Mr Jefferson, that this bank was set up simply to service the needs of the people in this valley. It would be a punishment to the other investors if we squandered our resources on a business that might still go under.'

Dagg glared at Deacon. 'You know my ranch is sound. You can have your money if you wait a few more weeks.'

'Sorry.'

'No bank would foreclose on a good operation,' said Charlie. 'I've never known one yet that wasn't interested in getting its money back. You'd rather ruin my father than give him a few weeks leeway?'

'That's the decision of the investors back East. Nothing I can do about it.'

'How much is the debt?' Charlie asked.

'In total, just under twelve thousand dollars. Due in five days. After that you'll be removed from the ranch.'

'I'll accompany the sheriff to ensure the eviction is carried out,' said Gus Tarleton.

'You'll never have the satisfaction of setting foot on Jefferson range again,' said Charlie.

CHAPTER SEVEN

Moments later Dagg and Charlie were out on the street, Dagg growling at the injustice of Brent Deacon's decision and Charlie talking low, trying to reassure his father that the money would be found to repay the loan but not wanting to explain how it could be done while they were yet in Tatanka Crossing. They were barely clear of the bank building when their attention was drawn to some kind of ruckus further down the street.

'It's John,' said Dagg, and he began to hurry ahead to discover the reason for the commotion. Charlie was a step behind.

A group had gathered on the boardwalk a short distance from where Charlie and his father had left John and Lucy Kincaid. Among them Charlie recognized the red and blue shirts of Hank Swales and Seth Woodlow, the men he had fought the previous day. Beyond, leaning against a Last Dollar balcony support post, the young deputy lounged, trying to look uninterested in the argument, as though it was nothing more than a tussle between boys in the schoolyard. Lucy Kincaid was holding John's arm, attempting to draw him away from the argument. John wore a bemused expression, as if he'd found himself in a situation that was beyond his comprehension but from which a sense of self-worth denied him the choice of walking away.

John's adversary was Zach Prescott. Free of the intoxication of last night's whiskey but still ensnared by the coil of lies and innuendo that Gus Tarleton had cast with regard to Charlie's involvement in the escape of Lars Svensson, Zach's demeanour demonstrated every fault in his character. His upper body was thrust forward so that his face was mere inches from John's, his words were being delivered with a spray of saliva, highlighting the anger and venom he put into the confrontation. At that moment he was repeating the resentment nurtured by the father because the youngest son had not returned from the war.

'Time to forget the war, Zach,' John told him. 'It's over. Charlie's back to help on the ranch. Nobody is looking for trouble with your family.'

'Well, trouble is what he's got if he hangs around here. He should keep on riding. Same goes for all you Jeffersons.'

'You've had too much to drink, Zach. Go home.'

Nervously, Lucy pulled again at John's arm, her eyes pleading with him to walk away; the unease she felt was a reflection of every townperson's belief that, following the attack on the Humboldt wagon and the death of Jed Prescott, the threat of even greater violence stalked the streets of Tatanka Crossing. Many citizens now avoided the thoroughfare and all had become careful of whom they spoke to and what they said, while the saddle tramps and gun hawks who had recently arrived in town had taken over, dominating the boardwalks with contemptuous swagger. Everyone agreed that whatever evil business had drawn them to the valley, it was now close at hand.

But Lucy's desire to draw John away from the confrontation wasn't solely based on imagination and

61

conjecture. It was apparent that John was determined to face up to Zach, whose hot-headed temperament had already earned him an unpopular reputation in the valley. Furthermore, on this day Zach unlike John, was armed, his left arm crooked so that his hand hovered close to the dull walnut handle of the Colt riding high on his left hip. Now he was throwing more words at John, attempting to use the events of yesterday to justify the weapon he carried; hoping perhaps, to lure John into an indiscretion that would allow him to use the gun.

'Your brother's fast with a gun, they say. Well, he doesn't frighten me. I could beat the dust out of him when we were younger and I can do it now.'

'You always talked a good fight, Zach, but I never saw you win one,' said John.

'John!' Lucy pulled at him again.

Zach grinned, thinking he'd found a weak point at which to attack. 'You gonna hide behind the pretty lady, John?'

'I'm not hiding, Zach. I'm here.'

Someone in the small crowd shouted. 'His brother used a girl to help Jed's killer escape . . .' but the voice trailed away as Charlie pushed through the mêlée.

Charlie pointed at the man; it was Hank Swales. 'Any time you choose to continue yesterday's discussion I'm ready for you,' he said. It didn't escape his notice that Seth Woodlow had moved a little way to the left so that the threesome, Zach, Hank and Seth, now faced him in a tri-angle. Charlie took a pace to his left, then another so that he could keep them all in his view. He spoke to Zach. 'Take it easy, Zach. There's no need for you to die today.'

Charlie's sudden appearance and his apparent cer-tainty of success in any confrontation with Hank Swales had sent out a clear message to Zach: this was a man who was no stranger to dealing out death. A line of sweat spread above his top lip. His eyes widened as he noted the easy way Charlie Jefferson stood, his arms hanging loose at his side, knowing himself, sure of his ability to draw his gun faster than any man here. If anyone was going to kill Charlie Jefferson he would have to have his gun clear of the holster before Charlie even knew he was in a duel. Zach's gaze slid towards Hank Swales and Seth Woodlow. According to Gus Tarleton they had been eager members of yesterday's posse. Now, as they edged out to a wider angle, he hoped he could depend on their support if he made a play.

Charlie Jefferson was talking, telling his brother to get Lucy Kincaid off the street. 'Your argument is with me, Zach,' he called, 'not my brother, but before you go reaching for that iron you should know that I've been out to the Circle P. I've spoken to your father. There's no need for a feud between us. Amos was my friend. I didn't want him to die.'

Sweat now beaded Zach's brow. He wanted to shout '*liar*' because his father's hatred of Charlie Jefferson was boundless; if Charlie Jefferson had gone to the Circle P he would never have ridden off alive. But if he called Charlie a liar he would be forced to go through with the gunfight. Now that they stood face to face he knew he couldn't win. He would be killed. It was clear that Charlie Jefferson was no stranger to such encounters. The way he spoke, the relaxed manner of his stance convinced Zach that he had talked himself into a situation from which he couldn't escape. His mind was a fog. No matter how he struggled he couldn't find a thought that would produce a face-saving back-down, or a word that would still Charlie's hand.

'Get your horse,' Charlie advised. 'Go home.'

63

Zach hesitated.

Hank Swales spoke. 'Don't let him order you about, Zach. He's already killed one brother and helped the killer of another. He'll try chasing you out of the territory if you don't stop him.'

Charlie turned so that he was full face with Hank Swales, half-turned away from Zach. 'Whoever you are, you should have learned your lesson yesterday.'

'Perhaps yesterday you should have kept your nose out of our business.' Seth Woodlow's voice caused Charlie to turn a little more.

'You figuring to take a hand in this argument?' Charlie asked.

'Not me,' said Seth. He folded his arms high across his chest as if to signify he was a non-combatant. 'I don't get involved in other people's fights. Just let them get on with it.'

An emphasis was placed on the last four words that made them sound like an order, alerting Charlie to Zach's play. His father's shouted warning occurred almost simultaneously. Zach had begun to draw his gun while Charlie's attention was distracted by the comments of the other two men. His weapon was clear of its holster when Charlie reacted to the warning, but still Zach wasn't quick enough Charlie spun to his left, drawing his Colt, pointing it at Zach and firing in one sweeping, fluid movement. His bullet smacked into Zach's left shoulder, spinning him backwards and dumping him on to the dusty street.

Amid shouts of surprise from those gathered around, Charlie swung his arm back so that his gun was levelled between Hank Swales and Seth Woodlow. Pistol cocked, he watched the pair, ready to react to a movement from either.

'Put up your gun,' someone ordered. It was the young

deputy, stepping forward with his own pistol extended, trying to cover every movement on the street.

'Arrest him, Brad,' suggested Hank Swales. 'Shot poor Zach.'

'Poor Zach asked for it,' said the deputy. He turned his attention to Charlie. 'But I don't want any more bloodshed on the street. Put your gun away. It was self-defence.'

Charlie complied slowly, unsure how much faith he had in the deputy after he'd berated him over his handling of yesterday's situation. But the deputy was ordering everybody to clear the street and go about their business. Charlie walked across to where Zach lay moaning in the dust. There was a lot of blood spreading over his shirt, front and back, but Charlie didn't think it was a lethal wound. He hadn't intended it to be so. He collected the gun that Zach had dropped and handed it to the deputy.

'Better get him to a doctor,' he said. The deputy gave that job to Hank and Seth, who threw looks at him which needed no interpretation.

Further along the street Charlie espied Brent Deacon with Gus Tarleton. It was clear that they had observed the brief outburst of violence. Tarleton's expression was cold, as though he were studying an intricate problem. Deacon on the other hand, when their eyes met, appeared to smile.

John Jefferson escorted a pale Lucy Kincaid to her parent's eating place while Charlie and his father went along to the sheriff's office with Brad Keen. Although the deputy agreed it was self-defence it was still necessary to record the incident and complete a report. Although the deputy's intervention hadn't been required, Charlie was nonetheless grateful for it. It was better to have the law present at these incidents, especially when the facts were otherwise likely to be misrepresented and distorted in favour of an opponent.

'Least I could do,' said Brad Keen. 'If I'd acted more like a lawman yesterday you wouldn't have become embroiled in what took place. It won't happen again.'

Half an hour later, with all formalities completed, Dagg and John headed for home while Charlie made his way to Doc Minchin's to see what damage had been done to Zach. As he approached the house the door opened. A young woman, elegant in a blue velvet dress and white shawl, stepped on to the veranda. Her hair was the corn yellow that Charlie had kept in his mind during the deprivations of winters on the march and summers under fire, and her eyes were a softer blue than he remembered as he'd waited for sleep to rescue him from the bitter night in line camps and dug-in redoubts. Her lips were coloured and her nose, unlike those of the male members of the Prescott family, was slim and straight. She stopped in her tracks when she saw and recognized Charlie. There was no pleasure in her expression.

Charlie removed his hat. 'You're looking well, Ruth,' he said. Prosperous was the word he felt he should use because her clothes and manner were far removed from his remembrance of her. She had always favoured dresses but nothing as splendid as the one she now wore. It put him in mind of the rig outs worn by society women down in New Orleans and it occurred to him that Ruth was the wife of a banker and therefore a society woman of Tatanka Crossing. 'I've come to see how Zach's doing.'

'He's got a hole in him,' she answered. 'But you would know that.'

'Ruth! The fight wasn't my idea.'

'No more than taking Amos off to war.'

Ruth's attitude surprised Charlie. 'No need for us to be enemies, Ruth. We'll be bumping into each other around town now that I'm back. We Jeffersons aren't the feuding kind.'

Ruth lifted her head an inch, haughtily. 'There won't be much point in staying around here when you lose your land.'

'We aren't going to lose our land,' he told her, his voice holding a harder edge than he had ever expected to use when conversing with Ruth. 'Like I told your husband and the sheriff, nobody is taking anything from our land.'

'It's the law,' she declared. 'Everybody knows that if you can't pay your mortgage you forfeit your land.'

'We can pay our mortgage,' stated Charlie, angry now that the girl whose memory had helped him survive the war should treat him with such coldness, should invoke in him such hostility. 'Tell your husband he'll have his money by the end of the week.' A momentary stab of anger scorched the pit of Charlie's stomach like a cut from a hot blade. His intention had been to turn up at the bank with the necessary payment and drop the cash on Brent Deacon's desk knowing what an unpleasant surprise it would be for the banker. But the words had been spoken and couldn't be taken back.

Charlie replaced his hat. 'I hope Zach's soon back in the saddle.' He turned to leave but stopped before stepping down from the porch. 'Just so you know,' he said, 'I wasn't trying to kill Zach. If that had been my intention he would be dead now.'

CHAPTER EIGHT

With the stubby index finger of his right hand Taub
Svensson tamped the rough shreds of baccy into the bowl
of his clay pipe. His brow was creased with deep lines, as
though preparing an after-dinner smoke was the most
important and most complex job he'd ever undertaken.
Charlie Jefferson and he were down at the large corral
looking over some of his stock as they milled around in
the declining heat of the day.

Charlie had kept his promise to Jenny and had ridden
across to the Svensson spread to share their evening meal.
They had greeted him warmly, all three waiting on the
veranda as he approached their home. Taub and his wife
had been particularly effusive, ushering him indoors with
smiles and words that would not have been out of place if
he had been a visiting President of the United States of
America rather than the homecoming son of their
neighbour.

Jenny's reception was, he thought, a little less warm; she
had stood a couple of paces behind her parents as though
reluctant to show any of the sparkle that had so marked
her attitude towards him when they'd first met. However,
she'd put on a blue dress which completely destroyed the
image of the dusty tomboy he'd carried with him from the

previous day, and when he told her how pretty she was she had found it impossible to maintain a stern attitude.

Confirmation that Charlie's visit was an occasion of pleasure for the Svenssons was provided when the food was served up on Mrs Svensson's best plates. They kept him talking throughout the meal, prising from him those details of his years away that were suitable topics to share in mixed company. Jenny spoke little but her eyes seldom strayed from his face as he described people he'd met and places he'd seen.

Now, she and her mother were clearing away the aftermath of the meal while Charlie and her father took a stroll around the horse enclosure; it was as they approached the herd that Charlie raised the matter of Lars and the killing of Jed Prescott.

Taub's drawn-out performance with the pipe was, of course, a strategy to collect his thoughts and formulate a reply. He needed to be sure that nothing he said in answer to Charlie Jefferson's question would compromise his son. Although he'd lived in America for almost twenty years, his use of the English language still fell far short of perfection, and at moments like this, when under stress to make his meaning clear, he was prone to use the wrong word, phrase or pronunciation.

Experience had taught him that careful consideration of what he wanted to say saved him the embarrassment of being misunderstood. Wherever possible he took the time to rehearse his speech in his head before giving wind to it. When he did speak, the words came out slowly, deliberately, as though the listener needed to be given an equal amount of time to savour his selected words. His voice was light and rich with his native Swedish accent. It was exactly as Charlie remembered it, almost musical, so that no matter how serious the content of his dialogue it was

69

difficult to believe that the soft-spoken Scandinavian was ever angry.

Even so, despite his placid nature, there was often something in the delivery of his words and the sharp glint in his blue eyes that reflected the true mark of a pioneer; stubbornness and determination.

'My boy has done nothing wrong,' he declared.

Charlie gave a slight shrug of his shoulders, a gesture meant to convey that such a statement had been unnecessary. 'He'll only prove his innocence if he surrenders to the sheriff. Running and hiding is a trait of the guilty.'

'Lars is not guilty. He did not kill Jed Prescott. But he cannot surrender to the sheriff.'

'You don't think he'll get a fair trial?'

'They will kill him before he is allowed to speak. Already they have tried.'

Taub's concern for his son's safety was understandable, but Charlie was no wiser about the events that had led up to the accusation of murder. He pressed Taub for the full story and slowly the details were imparted.

Jed and Lars had been haggling over the sale of a big black saddle horse for several days, Jed working on his friendship with Lars to have the price reduced and Lars arguing that the horse belonged to his father, thus removing any possible latitude with regard to the price.

'It was always the same,' Taub declared. 'Jed followed the same ritual every time he wanted one of my horses. It was a game between them but eventually he would pay the asking price because he knew I wouldn't cheat him. Everyone knows that only horses sound in wind and limb leave Taub Svensson's ranch.'

'But something went wrong this time?'

'According to witnesses, Lars and Jed met in the Last Dollar that night. Several people overheard their first few words while they drank at the bar. They were discussing the horse; squabbling about the price. Then they took a table at the back of the room, talking quietly together. When they finished their drinks they left the saloon. Moments later gunshots were heard. Jed was dead in the street and my son was fleeing the town. Two men claimed they had seen Lars shoot Jed Prescott without warning, not even giving him the chance to draw his pistol. They'd tried to stop Lars, firing at him so that he had no chance to explain what had happened, but he escaped.'

'Who witnessed the shooting?'

'Two men I don't know. They are new to the valley. They are the sort who hang around the Last Dollar all day but don't work cattle on any of the ranches around here.'

'Do you know their names?'

'Seth Woodlow and Hank Swales.'

Charlie knew these to be the men with whom he'd tangled twice since arriving in Tatanka Crossing. 'And the sheriff believes their story?'

Taub nodded. 'He, too, was firing his gun as Lars rode out of town. Trying to kill my boy, Charlie.'

Charlie Jefferson rubbed his jaw. It was clear from Taub's expression that he thought the situation hopeless, yet to jump to the conclusion that Lars wouldn't be treated fairly by Sheriff Simms if he gave himself up seemed to be a hasty conclusion if it was based solely on the sheriff's attempt to prevent him leaving town. That was the sheriff's job: to apprehend those suspected of breaking the law. If Taub had other reasons for suspecting that his son would come to harm while in the custody of the law it could only be because of something Lars had told him. 'What is Lars's version of what happened?'

Taub's head came up sharply, as if surprised by Charlie's question. 'What makes you think I've spoken to Lars?'

71

'Because he was here yesterday. Didn't Jenny tell you I'd seen their ruse to avoid the posse?'

'Posse?' The bewilderment in Taub's voice seemed genuine enough. Charlie described what he'd witnessed along the banks of the Feather Waters and the incident in Tatanka Crossing. 'My Jenny?'

'Look, Taub, those people are determined to get Lars. Some of them are probably watching us now, keeping an eye on the place in case he turns up here again. They'll catch on to Jenny's scheme and she won't get away with it again.'

'Lars and Jenny,' Taub said, reflectively. 'They are very close. Twins, you understand, it's like they have the same thoughts at the same time.'

'Doesn't mean they have to get killed together.' Charlie's words were deliberately brutal in order to convey the seriousness of the situation.

At that moment Jenny emerged from the house. She had changed into range garb: trousers and plaid shirt, as though she had chores to do about the ranch, but the hat and gloves she carried clarified her intention. She was going to run Collie before the last light of the day was gone. Free of the formality of a dress she was altogether more relaxed. She walked with a confident stride, her arms moving with a natural swing, her overall demeanour more relaxed than it had been earlier. Her eyes shone brightly, a betrayal of the mischief in her spirit that had been so evident the previous day, but the burgeoning smile died when her father called her to his side and without preamble scolded her for the risk she had taken to fool the posse.

'I can take care of myself,' she declared, 'and right now Lars needs our help.'

'Charlie says they were shooting at you,' her father said.

'Charlie should mind his own business,' snapped Jenny.

'Jenny! That's no way to behave. Charlie is worried that you will get hurt. Aren't you Charlie?'

Jenny found it difficult to look at Charlie because she knew that if he hadn't interfered the previous day she might well have got hurt and perhaps arrested for aiding her brother. What help would she be to Lars then, she wondered, if she was in jail? But Charlie's voice held no trace of rebuke when he spoke. 'You're right, Jenny,' he said. 'Lars does need help. If he is innocent it must be proved.'

'Of course he's innocent.' The sharpness of her retort angered her. She didn't want to speak angrily to Charlie Jefferson but inside she experienced such a mix of feelings that it had become a struggle to sort out the right response. She liked Charlie Jefferson; had liked him ever since she was eleven years old and had watched him win races during the spring and autumn get-togethers when only the seven families remained in the valley; had liked him right up to the time when it was generally accepted that Ruth Prescott was his girl. She could never explain why her stomach felt as empty as a rain barrel in summer when she saw them together, nor why she'd cried herself to sleep at night when he'd gone off to war.

But when she'd met him yesterday she'd known, and knowing that truth meant that she didn't want him to doubt her brother's innocence, nor did she want him to see her father scold her like a schoolgirl. She didn't want Charlie to think that she needed protecting, but she had loved the sensation in her stomach when her father had told her that Charlie was worried she'd get hurt.

'Then the best help we can give him is to prove it. He can't run and hide for ever. You've been brave and resourceful, Jenny,' Charlie said, 'but there is a price on his head that makes him a target for any man with a rifle. It will only be safe for him to return home when his name has been cleared. If he's innocent I'd like to help prove it.'

'Why?' Jenny asked.

'Because that's the way things have always been done in this valley; one family helping another.' He paused, his gaze lingering on her face as though memorizing the details. 'Besides,' he continued, 'I'm not sure that my father's troubles are unconnected with yours. Tatanka Crossing has changed while I've been away and I figure to understand why.'

'Charlie's right,' said Taub reflectively. 'You're right, Charlie. What can we do?'

'First you need to tell me Lars's side of the story.'

As it happened, there wasn't much to tell. The conversation in the Last Dollar between Lars and Jed Prescott had not only been about the purchase of the black saddle horse. Jed had unearthed some information and as they sat at the table at the back of the saloon, had confided in Lars. Outside, they had crossed the street to the rail where their horses were tied.

Without warning, shots were fired and Jed fell. Because Lars had been between horses he'd avoided the first fusillade and had been able to escape by clinging to the side of his mount. But he'd recognized the men, Swales and Woodlow, and had heard their shouts, accusing him as Jed's murderer so that those emerging from the saloon and mercantile took up the cry that Lars Svensson had killed Jed Prescott.

Lars had seen Sheriff Simms on the boardwalk as he'd vaulted on to his horse, and the lapse of time between that and the killing of Jed Prescott made it seem probable that he had witnessed the shooting or been involved in it, which was why Lars wasn't prepared to surrender to the

74

law in Tatanka Crossing.

Charlie thought that the information Jed had uncovered was probably a significant pointer to his murder, but Taub was unable to satisfy his curiosity when he asked about it. Lars had not passed anything on to his father, figuring it was safer for his family if they didn't know what he knew. Charlie wasn't of the same opinion. If it was important enough for someone to kill once, then those who were anxious to keep the secret would kill again.

'Where is Lars hiding?' Charlie asked.

'Up in the north wash,' Taub said.

'That old trapper's cabin?' Charlie remembered it. It had been little more than an unsafe collection of logs when they'd settled in the valley all those years ago. He could only imagine what sort of dilapidated state it was in now but, what was more important, if Ezra Prescott ever started thinking clearly he would identify it as a likely refuge for a man on the run. 'He can't stay there. I still think his best chance is to surrender to the law.'

'He won't put himself in the hands of Sheriff Simms.'

Charlie offered a solution. 'I'm riding to Laramie tomorrow. Lars can come with me and tell his story to the territorial marshal. Lars will be safer in Laramie than he is alone in that cabin, and the marshal will conduct an honest investigation into the death of Jed Prescott.'

The suggestion wasn't greeted with Taub's wholehearted agreement. The prospect of having his son under lock and key while a lawman came to Tatanka Crossing to hear the testament of his accusers frightened him. Everyone in Tatanka Crossing had heard the story of Jed Prescott's slaying and it was common knowledge that Sheriff Simms had sent out a posse to capture Lars, dead or alive. With such a weight of opinion against his son it was difficult to see how another lawman could come to any other conclusion than to charge Lars with murder.

Charlie Jefferson offered the other side of the argument: that the marshal's investigation would be centred
on whatever information Lars had been given by Jed
Prescott. That information, Charlie insisted, would prove
Lars Svensson's innocence but until it was made available
to the law, Lars would remain a fugitive. Gradually, Taub
ran out of resistance and it was agreed that Charlie would
ride to the north wash early the following morning and
persuade Lars to accompany him to Laramie.

Jenny had not spoken during their discussion. She
shared her father's misgivings but the intensity of Charlie's
argument gave her confidence in him. She wanted her
brother home and she was convinced that he needed to
prove his innocence to make that possible. 'I'll take you to
him,' she said. 'You'll need me if you hope to get close to
him. From a distance, Lars won't recognize you. He'll take
you for a bounty hunter and be gone from the cabin
before you get within a mile of it.' Charlie could see sense
in the suggestion and readily agreed. 'Now,' she added,
'I'm going to ride Collie up to Bull Creek while there is
still some light in the day.' She flashed a look that was both
shy and inviting, then crossed the yard to the stable. A few
moments later she galloped off across the stretch of
meadow that separated the ranch from the low western
slopes.

Charlie bade farewell to Taub and his wife and
promised to bring news of Lars as soon as he returned
from Laramie. The trail to Bull Creek took him some
miles out of his way home but Jenny's parting glance had
lodged in his mind and he wanted to see her again.

He came across her by the white rock, a landmark on a
crest looking west across the Tatanka as it made its way
from Tatanka Crossing to the junction with the Platte. She

was sitting on a branch of an old willow which had reached out and dipped until it almost touched the ground before making one last effort to reach skywards again. The pinto was grazing behind her, the long lead rein thrown carelessly over the branch.

She didn't turn at the sound of Charlie's arrival, kept her gaze focused on the blue/pink distant horizon. He didn't sit, instead he lounged against the trunk, held the reins of the pony he'd borrowed from his father, which stood silently and motionless at his side.

'This is my favourite place,' said Jenny. 'Perhaps one day I'll have a home built here.'

Charlie studied the site. Perhaps nearer the river with the crest behind the building to give it shelter from the morning heat. But in the evening, sitting on a porch watching the setting sun, it would be a fine place.

'Do you ever think of having a home, Charlie?'

Ruth had talked about it with him, had had a location in mind on her father's land. Not unlike this one, but Charlie had never thought about it as their home. It had been the site of their ranch house, a place for conducting the business of running cattle, which was what, at that time, he'd envisaged his future life to be.

'I saw you in town today,' Jenny said, not waiting for an answer. 'Saw your fight with Zach Prescott. Why do the Prescotts blame you for Amos's death?'

Charlie had never got the answer to that straight in his own head. 'I guess some people just need a target for their anger.' A small frown of incomprehension showed between Jenny's eyes. Charlie tried to explain further. 'Ezra's the kind of man for whom fighting is a personal thing. Something he'd do only for his own protection or gain. The only way he can make sense of Amos joining the army is by believing that I persuaded him to disobey his father.'

'Will he ever stop hating you?'

'I don't suppose we'll ever be friends but I'm hopeful that there won't be any more violence between our families.' He told her of his visit to the Circle P that morning and how unnecessary Zach's confrontation had been.

'You were fast with your gun,' Jenny said. 'I overheard people say that to be so fast you must have killed a lot of people.'

'Jenny!' Charlie spoke softly. Gunfighting and killing weren't subjects he wanted to discuss with Jenny.

'Have you, Charlie? Have you killed men?'

'Jenny!' he repeated.

'I'm not frightened of you, Charlie.' She walked towards him, stood toe to toe and looked up into his eyes. 'I hope you have, because I'm afraid for Lars. He isn't a fighter, not in that way, and if you are going to protect him all the way to Laramie I want to be sure you can do it.'

'I'll do everything I need to.'

She didn't doubt that; she could sense the strength of Charlie Jefferson and his ability to survive. She wanted to put her hands on his arms to know his strength, wanted to rest her head against his chest to know his comfort. Instead, she spoke again, uttering words that had been inside since yesterday when he'd stopped on the ridge above Tatanka Crossing, words she had no right to give air to. 'What about Ruth?'

'Ruth?'

'Marrying Brent Deacon! Aren't you angry? Don't you hate her?'

Jenny's forthright questions surprised Charlie, especially as they were asked in a voice strained with emotion. 'Well,' he began, drawling the word while he decided how best to answer. It took only a second to decide that a forthright question deserved an honest reply. 'It's fair to say I wasn't happy when I first heard the news, especially when I'd already formed a poor opinion of the man she'd chosen, but I had no right to expect her to wait for me. I've been away six years. People change in that time and if you are not there to change with them I guess you can grow in different directions.

'So I'm not angry and I certainly don't hate her. It wouldn't be possible to hate her, Jenny. She was the one who got me through the war. War isn't pretty. You see things and do things you never think possible and you feel inhuman, ashamed and frightened, and after a battle when you've survived but can't cheer a victory because you're not sure who has won, you feel sick for being grateful that there are more dead in the ranks of your enemy.

'That's when you need something to keep your sanity and deflect thoughts of desertion. I thought of Ruth. Without the ability to conjure up her face I would have gone mad. So no, pray God I never hate her.'

Jenny's head drooped so that Charlie wouldn't see the wetness in her eyes. 'I wish . . .' she murmured, 'I wish. . . .' Then her forehead was against his chest and the rest of her words were whispered to her feet.

'What do you wish, Jenny?' Charlie held her upper arms and eased her away. She shook her head. He took hold of her chin and lifted it so that, unwillingly, she was once again looking at his face. 'What do you wish?'

'I wish I had been the one you'd thought of after a battle.'

CHAPTER NINE

While Charlie Jefferson was sharing a meal with the Svensson family, Brent Deacon was entertaining Henry 'Tex' McFadden and Seymour Brewster. Instead of being in the back room of the Last Dollar where they regularly met, they were in the parlour of the home Deacon had had built at the far end of town. They met here when they had matters to discuss which were not for the ears of Sheriff Simms or Lawyer Carter and, in addition this night, he'd sent his wife on an errand and wanted to be home when she returned.

Tex McFadden was a bull of a man who had worked in lumber camps since his youth He had undertaken all manner of jobs and had reached this peak in his career by being knowledgeable, resourceful and strong enough to let those he employed know that anything they could do he could do better. So, although Brent Deacon was the senior man in this triumvirate, Buster spoke freely because he knew no other way.

'I've got a lot of strong men up at the camp,' he declared, 'men capable of snapping other men in two, but they aren't gunfighters. If this Jefferson fellow is as fast as rumour has it then I've got nobody I can put on the street to face him. I expect it is the same with Seymour.'

He looked at the mine manager for agreement, which was duly forthcoming. 'As long as he can sit on a horse and swing a rope,' continued Tex, 'a gunfighter can pass himself off as a ranch hand. They don't blend in so easily as mine workers or loggers.'

'I didn't specify the manner of Jefferson's killing,' said Deacon. 'If it's a face-to-face duel on Main Street then all well and good, but any other means will still suit our purpose.'

Neither McFadden nor Brewster responded quickly. Both men were reluctant to criticise the implication in Deacon's words. They both knew the calibre of the men who worked for them: rough, sometimes brutal in the way they fought with other men, but rarely in secret, preferring witnesses around to attest to their victory. Any suggestion of ambush would be regarded as cowardice, incurring the endless contempt of fellow workers.

'Someone who'll assist Gus Tarleton,' added Deacon. 'One of you must know someone who'll do a job for fifty dollars!'

Brewster knew one or two who were always short of money, men who lost their wages too easily at the gaming table. If they didn't have to pull the trigger they might be prepared to act as decoy for Tarleton, but he wasn't yet ready to volunteer their names. 'You're sure this Jefferson fellow is going to cause trouble?' he asked Deacon.

'He's interfered twice already and he told Ruth he has the means of paying off his father's debt. We can't let that happen. Breaking Dagg Jefferson's resistance, getting his land, is the key to gaining control of the valley.'

'Do you think he knows why the company wants this valley?'

Brent Deacon shook his head. 'Impossible,' he declared. 'What could he know? Nobody even knows that we're all employed by Cincinnati Enterprises. No, he doesn't know anything yet but he's already proved that he's not a man to stand aside and let things happen. If he begins to concern himself in our affairs he could become troublesome.'

'Like your brother-in-law did,' murmured Seymour Brewster.

Deacon threw him an angry look, suspecting the mine manager was being critical of him. It had been his own negligence that had put Jed Prescott in possession of knowledge he should not have had. Jed had read some correspondence left on his unattended desk, correspondence which made Brent's purpose in the valley abundantly clear and which was as threatening to the Prescott ranch as it was to every other landowner in the valley.

Cincinnati Enterprises, who had made two unsuccessful attempts to buy out the ranchers, were now playing a more devious game and Brent Deacon was their chief agent, set with the task of freeing the land from the hands of the current owners and buying it up as cheaply as possible on behalf of the company. The business men back East had known that the achievement of this plan would take many months and had been prepared to wait, but now, more than a year after Deacon's arrival at Tatanka Crossing, not one acre of land was yet owned by their company. Now, they were pushing their man for results.

In his mind, Brent Deacon had a clear strategy, the implementation of which had been made easier by two separate factors. First, he had falsely gained the confidence of the ranchers by replacing Sam Flint. Such had been their reliance on Flint's offices that it had taken many months for them to realize that Deacon was not acting on their behalf. By the time Dagg Jefferson, Taub

Svensson and Tommy Humboldt realized that they needed to make their own arrangements they were barely able to meet their obligations. His latest swindle, announcing that the army no longer wanted them to supply beef, had put the two cattle ranchers in serious financial trouble. In fact, the army had made no such proclamation. Deacon was supplying the full quota of beef from the Prescott ranch.

The second factor in his favour was his marriage with Ruth Prescott. It was easy for him to convince everyone, including Ruth, that their courtship and marriage were based on love. Ruth was a beautiful girl, a wife to make any man proud, but Deacon needed her for two reasons, neither of which had anything to do with romance.

One of them was the Prescott ranch, one of the two most powerful in the valley. Deacon wanted the land as a personal bonus. With his knowledge of its true value, he intended to sell it to his employers at top dollar, but only after he'd secured for them the rest of the valley at a minimum price. Jed Prescott was already dead, killed at his insistence but the blame for it conveniently steered in another direction.

Deacon had no reason to suppose that a similar fate couldn't be arranged for Ezra Prescott and his one remaining son. Then Ruth would inherit it all and, as husband and banker he would ensure that the deeds of the ranch were transferred into his name so that he could dispose of the land as swiftly as possible. He hadn't considered Ruth's fate after that. Perhaps he would take her with him when he left the valley. After all, when Charlie Jefferson had been taken care of, she wouldn't be able to seek solace in the arms of her childhood sweetheart.

The Jeffersons had been the other reason for his marriage. Dagg Jefferson was an important man in the valley,

83

the sort of man who would resist any attempted takeover and to whom the others would turn in time of trouble. Marriage to Ruth had been a means of increasing the hostility between the two families although, from his observations, that hostility had never been two-way. Fortunately, his suggestion that Cincinnati Enterprises should act as backers for the small Tatanka Crossing bank had provided him with all the leverage he needed to ruin Dagg Jefferson.

'Yes, like my brother-in-law,' he declared. In many ways he considered Brewster a weak man, certainly not brave enough to challenge his authority or methods. 'That knowledge in the right hands could unite the ranchers in their opposition to the company's plan to buy up the land.'

Tex McFadden spoke. 'That kid they are blaming for the killing, do you think he knows what was in the letters?'

'Can't do.' Deacon's voice held a note of certainty. 'He'd have passed on what he knows by now and there would be whispers around town. Have you heard anything?'

Both McFadden and Brewster shook their heads. All the talk they'd heard was that the young Svensson kid was an unlikely killer, but nobody had come forward with any proof that he hadn't killed Jed Prescott.

At that moment the door opened and Ruth Deacon, looking elegant in a long, bottle-green travel coat and small black hat, entered. Her husband crossed the room, took her arms and kissed her lightly on the cheek as though her absence had put him through torment.

'I didn't expect you back so soon,' he said.

'He wasn't at home,' she answered. 'Dining with the Svensson family.'

'Then you learned nothing.'

Ruth removed her hat before answering, drawing a long pearl-topped pin from the hat and placing both on a polished table at the back of the room. 'The Jeffersons were surprised to see me,' she said.

Deacon would have been surprised if it had been otherwise but he kept his counsel; he sensed that his wife had more to say and wanted to disclose it in her own time.

'I hinted that I would return tomorrow to speak to Charlie but Mrs Jefferson said I would be wasting my time. He has business at Laramie.'

'Laramie!'

'Mr Jefferson gave his wife a flustered look when she told me that, as if she'd let slip something that was best kept secret.'

I can imagine, thought her husband as he ushered her into an adjoining room, assuring her that his business with McFadden and Brewster would soon be concluded.

Charlie Jefferson's trip to Laramie provided Brent with a double cause for concern. It was reasonable to assume that the rancher's son was unaware of the new bank in Tatanka Crossing and therefore had made arrangements for any wealth he'd amassed to be available through the Cattlemen's Bank. Perhaps he only had enough to cover the next month's mortgage payment, but any delay would prove fatal to Brent's ambition.

The other consideration was the nearness of the army outpost to Laramie. If Charlie Jefferson spoke with the colonel he would immediately uncover the truth about the cattle contract. 'Get Gus Tarleton,' he told Seymour Brewer.

Tarleton had been waiting on the porch in readiness for such a summons from his paymaster so was able to present himself before Deacon almost immediately. 'Which is the quickest route to Laramie from the Jefferson ranch?' Deacon asked him.

'Downstream to the big bend then south around Horn Hill.'

That description tallied with Deacon's knowledge of the area and there was no dissent from the other two. 'Charlie Jefferson will be travelling that way tomorrow. He must not get to Laramie. Do I make myself clear?'

Gus Tarleton moved his head to signify that he understood. 'There's a good spot just approaching the hill. I'll see him coming for miles.'

'Get there early. He must not get past. Take Hank and Seth with you.'

'I can do the job alone,' said Gus. 'Besides, they'll be keeping an eye on the Svensson place.'

Deacon was about to insist; preventing Charlie Jefferson from reaching Laramie was more important at the moment than chasing the Svensson kid, who was probably no threat at all, but Tarleton had turned away, was heading for the door walking with a swagger that suggested both confidence and a desire to get the job done. 'Don't fail,' Deacon said. 'I want Charlie Jefferson dead.'

In the adjoining room, her ear pressed to the door as it had been during other meetings with Brewster and McFadden, Ruth Deacon heard her husband's words. By eavesdropping, she had gained snippets of information relating to her husband's activities. She knew, for instance, of his business association with Brewster, McFadden and Cincinnati Enterprises. She had gleaned that the valley was rich in minerals and that it was her husband's intention to obtain it at the cheapest price. She had brushed from her mind the fact that her own family's land was part of the valley, convincing herself that cheating her father would not be part of Brent's plan.

Now, instinctively, she recoiled at the bleakness of

Brent's instruction. Charlie Jefferson had been her first love and, momentarily, every instinct impelled her to seek mercy, but such charity didn't live long in her heart. Any feelings she might have had for the young man who had gone off to war with her brother six years ago, were little more than a flutter of memory.

Brent Deacon had come into her life as a complete man. Whatever experience he'd had before arriving in Tatanka Crossing he had since put to good use by becoming the wealthiest man in the settlement. He had made it clear to her that being the owner of an emporium, a saloon and a bank was only the beginning of his authority in this territory. Shortly after they were married he'd told her that one day soon the whole valley would be under his control.

She had no reason to doubt him for she knew he was unscrupulous. He cared for no other needs but his own and would do whatever was necessary to bring his plans to fruition. It was his single-mindedness as much as his money-making ability and debonair attitude that attracted her to him, and whatever he asked of her she was prepared to do.

That was why she'd driven out that evening to the Jefferson ranch. Brent had told her there was nothing to be gained by shunning Charlie Jefferson. Perhaps her father's enmity would never be overcome, but if Charlie intended staying on in Tatanka Crossing then a friendly visit now might prevent awkwardness in the future.

'Find out his plans,' Brent had told her. 'Perhaps he's returned with enough money to buy his own place. After all, Ruth, he did think he was coming home to marry you.'

So she'd gone, not because she believed the sentiments Brent had expressed but because she realized that any information extracted from Charlie Jefferson was important to her husband. No matter how much Charlie Jefferson had loved her in the past, she now realized he was not the kind of man who would have provided for her in the manner she had always wanted and to which she was now accustomed. Charlie Jefferson's roots were on the range and he was unlikely ever to leave it.

It had been almost four years since she'd last visited the Jefferson ranch, banned from it first of all by an angry father, then avoiding it after her marriage. Dagg and Mary Jefferson couldn't disguise their surprise and suspicion when she drove her one-horse buggy into their yard. She was invited into the house but never took a seat. Charlie's absence removed any need to loiter.

'Perhaps I'll see him tomorrow,' Ruth had said as she climbed back into the gig. That was when Mary Jefferson had uttered the remark about Charlie's business in Laramie, which in turn had evoked Dagg Jefferson's anxious look.

Ruth removed her coat and draped it over a chair. She looked around the room, savouring the furnishings and expensive knick-knacks provided by her husband. This was her life and Charlie Jefferson's return wasn't going to interfere with it. She recalled Brent's last words. *I want Charlie Jefferson dead.* Charlie Jefferson, it seemed, wasn't going to interfere with anything ever again.

CHAPTER TEN

Charlie and Jenny had lingered by the white rock for almost an hour after Jenny's blunt declaration of her wishes; she trying to recover a modicum of her lost reserve, and he anxious to retain her goodwill, nervous lest any embarrassment caused by her giving unexpected voice to her feelings for him should cause her to avoid his immediate company. But they had parted as friends and had agreed to meet at the same spot early next morning so that she could ride with him to the old trapper's cabin in the north wash.

His father was waiting on the small front porch when he rode in to the yard. He walked with him to the stable where he unsaddled and rubbed down the mare. Dagg talked about horses for a while but Charlie sensed an uneasiness in his father's manner, figuring he was still concerned about the repayment of the debt. Charlie had assured him that he had enough money in the Cattlemen's Bank at Laramie and that he intended withdrawing it the next day, but perhaps taking his son's money caused his father a different kind of anxiety.

'Funny how life moves in little circles,' he told Dagg.

'How so?' enquired his father.

'After the war I made a pact with myself that I wouldn't

89

come home until I had sufficient money to buy up some land for Ruth and me to have our own place. It took some time and I did some things that perhaps I wouldn't do again, but I got the money.'

Dagg had given him a strange look at that moment, curious as to how Charlie had amassed so much money, but this was the West and you didn't enquire into another man's business, not even if that man was your son.

'Don't worry, Pa,' Charlie said, 'I didn't do anything against the law.' In fact, he had done the opposite. At the end of the war, bands of renegade Confederate soldiers who had refused the terms of surrender had pillaged and robbed all over the mid-west states. Rewards were offered for their capture and Charlie saw it as an opportunity to get the money he desired. In hindsight, he had some sympathy for those soldiers of a defeated army. Hounding them, often to their deaths, was an inglorious end to an inglorious war. But the war had affected everyone in Kansas, Missouri and the surrounding states and the rebel bands were making war on those townspeople and farmers who were trying, peaceably, to reconstruct their own lives. They had to be stopped. The military depended on civilian intelligence to pinpoint the positions of the gangs. It was dangerous work, which accounted for the high bounties it attracted. Charlie had earned several and had deposited almost $15,000 in the Cattlemen's Bank at Laramie on his journey home.

'Now,' Charlie had continued, 'I'm going to use that money to spoil the plans of the husband of the girl I thought was going to be my bride.'

'One of life's ironies,' proclaimed Dagg. Then he coughed, a clearing of the throat that was the precursor to the words he needed to say. Inadvertently, Charlie had provided the opening for him to pass on the news he had found difficult to tell. 'She was here tonight. Ruth. Came to apologize for her behaviour earlier.'

Charlie wanted to feel some pleasure from the fact that Ruth had called to see him, but he could not. He remembered all too well their bitter encounter outside Doctor Minchin's office and he could not shake off the belief that she had come because he'd told her he could pay his father's debt. She had been seeking information for her husband. The expression on his father's face told him that he, too, had been wary of her visit.

'We let slip that you were going to Laramie tomorrow,' Dagg said.

Charlie shook his head. 'Don't worry, Pa. Nobody is going to do anything to take this land from us.'

Jenny Svensson was already at the white rock above the Tatanka when Charlie reached that point early next morning. If Charlie thought they'd parted as friends then the smile she bestowed hinted at something a great deal more. They exchanged greetings as Jenny approached the spot where Charlie dismounted. She stood close to him, looking up into his face, eyes wide and bright, lips soft and slightly parted and skin smooth, sun-burnished and tempting Charlie to touch. He knew she wouldn't object if he did, wouldn't repel him if he lowered his head and kissed her.

Two faces had occupied his mind for much of the night. Jenny's had been one because her declaration beside the white rock had left him bewildered. No matter how he'd struggled, he'd been unable to find an explanation for the feelings he'd aroused in her. He'd settled on the foolishness of young girls but he'd readily conceded that, in addition to being pretty and flushed with life, she was as brave and daring as many a man he'd come across during his travels.

The other face had been Ruth's, but he had not been able to recapture the image of her that had come nightly when death had been close at hand. It angered him that the face he saw was the one that had spoken bitter words and had presented false friendship to his parents. It wasn't the way he wanted to think of her, but it was, he realized, the way he always would.

So in the morning it was Jenny he thought of first and now she was here almost compelling him to grin with pleasure. Even so, he counselled himself that this was no time for dalliance. Jenny Svensson was a beautiful girl but helping her brother and saving his father's ranch were more important matters at the moment. There was trouble in the valley and the atmosphere he'd sensed since arriving home told Charlie that matters were coming to a head.

'Jenny,' he began, but the conversation went no further. From a nearby thicket came the whinny of a horse. Suddenly it emerged, rearing, stomping, eyes ablaze with inherent fear. The rider, the blue-shirted Seth Woodlow, began shouting in surprise, cursing his mount for almost throwing him but also for betraying his presence to Charlie and Jenny. The snorting horse rose again on its hindlegs, the forelegs clawing at the sky as it looked down, searching for sight of its natural enemy. A snake slithered through the grass, hastily avoiding the hoofs that smashed the ground around it.

Seth Woodlow, a guileless, brutal man drew his pistol and fired once, twice, three times before the final bullet splattered the head from the snake's body. He cursed his horse again although it was now more composed, turning in a circle around the dead creature.

Charlie Jefferson grasped the situation immediately.

This was confirmation that a constant watch was being held on the Svensson horse farm. Seth Woodlow, he surmised, had followed Jenny from her ranch, hoping she would lead him to her brother. While the rider attempted to control his spooked mount, Charlie raced across the grass and leapt at Seth. Ignoring the weapon, Charlie grabbed the arm which held the gun and pulled Seth from the back of the still flustered animal.

Although he'd taken Seth by surprise, disarming him wasn't an easy matter. Seth was strong and the two men struggled for possession of the gun for almost a minute. Charlie forced Seth's arm high so that any discharge of the weapon would be harmless. Through gritted teeth, an indication of the effort required for him to retain his grip on the pistol, Seth muttered curses and threats. Charlie saved his breath so that when the opportunity presented itself he was able to muster sufficient power into a right hook under the heart to send Seth sprawling on his back in the dust. Momentarily, the gun slipped from his clutch. He rolled, stretching out his left hand to grab it again. Charlie was quicker, grinding the heel of his boot over Seth's fingers, breaking at least two and provoking a sickening yell of pain. With his left hand, Charlie grabbed the front of Seth's shirt, pulled his head away from the ground and delivered a terrible punch with his right fist. Seth sagged, unconscious, and Charlie let him fall.

While Seth was still unaware of what was happening, Charlie bound him with his own rope and heaved him across the saddle. As he regained his senses, Seth found himself looking at the ground, secured to his mount by a rope which had been passed twice under the horse's belly.

'Stay away from the Svensson family,' Charlie ordered, 'or you'll answer to me. Lars didn't kill Jed Prescott and I intend to prove it.' Whatever answer Seth was going to give was driven out of him when his horse suddenly jumped forward, responding to Charlie's smack on its rump. For a moment Charlie and Jenny watched as the horse careered along the trail, the pack on its back looking awkward and rigid.

'Come on,' said Charlie. 'Get me to Lars while we know nobody is following us.'

The sun was bright but the full effect of its heat had yet to be realized. Even so, Charlie didn't set a punishing pace for the horses. He was conscious of the fact that reaching the shack where Lars was lying low was only the first part of his journey. Later he had to ride on to Laramie and although his father had vouched for the ability of the horse he'd borrowed it was still an unproven animal to Charlie.

They followed the Tatanka west for five miles, then cut northwards into the hill country, using a trail that had been formed over centuries by tribesmen and trappers. The discovery of Seth Woodlow had reminded Charlie of the seriousness of the situation in which Lars Svensson now found himself. It also made him aware of the danger that Jenny was in until her brother's innocence was proved. Much as he admired her persistence in championing his cause, he was nonetheless aware that they were dealing with people who were determined, at all costs, to prevent Lars from telling his version of events. If Jenny was caught with him then Charlie had no doubt that her life, too, would be forfeit. Accordingly, the thoughts and pleasure that had come over him when he'd reached the white rock were now driven completely from his mind.

Jenny held back her pinto with reluctance. Testing the speed and endurance of horses had long been the centre of her existence, and this morning, with Charlie Jefferson

94

for a companion, she was sure that riding the range at full gallop would prove the greatest joy of her life. The sudden explosion of violence at the white rock had had no negative effect on that expectation; it had, indeed, only served to assure her that in times of trouble Charlie Jefferson would not let her down. But she had noted his mood since putting spur to horse, had noticed the tight line of his mouth and took her cue from that. Charlie Jefferson wasn't seeking conversation so she remained quiet for most of the journey, only speaking when they reined in their mounts at the top of the slope that led down to her brother's hideaway shack.

The shack was exactly as Charlie remembered: small, one room with a roof that sloped dramatically from front to back, the rear of the structure almost touching the hillside behind. It was a construction of old, darkened timbers that, even at the distance from which they now viewed it, seemed too frail to provide any sort of protection from wind, rain or snow. Fortunately, those elements were still months away and had not been a concern for Lars.

It was an open hillside that descended to the building about half a mile away. There were no trees but a lush covering of meadow grass and wild flowers.

'He'll have spotted us by now,' Jenny said, and proceeded to wave an arm from side to side, a gesture which was intended to indicate that all was well. When she urged her horse forward, Charlie followed.

Lars didn't emerge from the shack. Instead they found him wedged in one of the dark corners, his rifle primed and aimed at Charlie's stomach when he came through the door.

'Lars,' his sister said, 'he's here to help.'

'Who is he?'

95

'Do you not recognize him? It's Charlie Jefferson.'

'Jefferson!' Lars moved nearer to the centre of the room. The similarity between him and his sister was striking, but whereas Jenny shone with vitality and determination, Lars appeared grey, anxious and unsure. 'How can you help me?'

'By persuading you to give yourself up to the law.'

Lars Svensson's eyes widened, an indication of his fear and a conviction that Charlie had somehow tricked his sister into betraying his hideout.

'Never,' he declared. 'They'll hang me. Sheriff Simms has already tried to kill me.'

'I'm not suggesting we go back to Tatanka Crossing. There's a Federal Marshal in Laramie. He'll listen to your story. I'm on my way there now. I'll make sure you get there safely.'

'Listen to him, Lars. He's talking sense. You can't hide here much longer. Eventually a posse or a bounty hunter will find you. There's a big reward for your capture.' Brother and sister exchanged looks. For his part it was clear that he was tired of being alone; that he needed guidance before taking another step; that his sister was a staff on which he readily leaned. 'You can trust Charlie,' she told him, offering a smile that compelled him to believe that all was now well.

It took another ten minutes to persuade Lars that going to Laramie was his best course of action, but doubts still lingered and they were refuelled when he learned that Jenny was not going with them. For a moment she seemed prepared to argue with Charlie for her inclusion in the trip, but he pointed out the worry that her unexplained absence would cause her parents and she relented immediately.

So they parted at the shack. Lars saddled his own pinto,

which was stabled in a cleft of the hillside almost behind the shack. Charlie looked at brother and sister and at the two horses.

'Don't wear your hat,' he told Jenny. 'Let your hair fly free. Make sure that everyone knows you're a girl. It might have been a good trick once to fool a posse that you were your brother but it could backfire on you. We don't want anyone mistaking you again for Lars.'

Jenny smiled. 'Worried about me, Charlie?'

Charlie didn't smile. 'Yes.'

Jenny removed her hat and brushed her fingers through her hair. 'You'll come to the ranch when you return?'

'I promised your father I would.'

A look of exasperation crossed the girl's face, but it didn't stay there long because Charlie yelled and swiped his hat at the pinto, causing it to run away up the hill.

Lars watched the little scene, an inkling of the relationship between Charlie Jefferson and his sister lodging in his mind. But it was Charlie who spoke. 'You can tell me what happened that night in Tatanka Crossing while we ride.'

Already, they were well west of Tatanka Crossing, so avoiding the settlement on the way south to Laramie was a simple matter. Being so far west also meant that their crossing of the Feather Waters was far upstream from Horn Hill and the bullet that awaited Charlie in Gus Tarleton's rifle. It was late morning when they set out, later than Charlie had intended, which probably meant they would arrive in Laramie too late for him to conduct the business that was the original purpose of his journey. However, before they arrived in Laramie, Lars had given Charlie the few details he had about events leading up to the killing of Jed Prescott.

97

It was pretty much as Taub had related over the evening meal, but hearing it first hand from Lars made Jed's agitation that night all the more vivid.

'I knew something was troubling him when we met in the Last Dollar. He wouldn't tell me what was wrong but kept casting glances around the room as though he suspected someone was watching us. Eventually he agreed to talk outside.

'We walked across the street to the rail where our horses were tied. Jed said he'd seen some papers on Brent's desk. Before he could give me any details a shot rang out and Jed fell against me. I tried to hold him but there was blood all over the back of his shirt and he slid to the ground. Another shot hit the post above my head and I heard someone shout that I'd killed Jed.

'At the same time I realized that there was someone standing close by on the boardwalk. It was Sheriff Simms. He told me to surrender. I guess I panicked. I was holding the reins of my horse and just leapt on his back and rode out of town. Several guns were fired at me and I could hear someone shouting: *The Svensson kid's killed Jed Prescott.* It's not true, Charlie. I didn't. I wasn't even carrying a gun.'

Jim Tozer, the federal marshal, listened carefully to everything Charlie and Lars told him, then shuffled through a handful of papers on his desk, dismissing them with a grunt. 'This happened more than a week ago?' he asked Lars. When he got an affirmative answer he pointed at the pieces of paper he'd thrown back on the desk. 'No notification that you are wanted in Tatanka Crossing. The first thing I'd expect Tom Simms to do would be to inform me of a murder.'

'It's like I say, Marshal,' said Charlie Jefferson. 'They don't mean to give Lars a trial. They'll hang him, for sure, if he returns to Tatanka Crossing. He needs to be locked up here for his own protection, and you need to come back with me to Tatanka Crossing to investigate the death of Jed Prescott.'

'Can't do either of those things,' drawled Jim Tozer. 'The boy isn't wanted here for anything so I can't lock him up. And there's a trial under way here in Laramie that might go another two days. I've got to be here. I'll get to Tatanka Crossing as soon as I'm able.'

Charlie spoke to Lars. 'Probably best if you stayed here at Laramie for a while. Take a room at the hotel. Use a different name. I'll get word to you when it is safe to return.'

For the moment it was the best advice Charlie could give. The expression on Lars Svensson's face made it difficult for Charlie to decide whether the boy was pleased that he wasn't to be held in prison or afraid that he would be alone in Laramie without any protection.

CHAPTER ELEVEN

Not altogether by chance it was his partner, Hank Swales, who, around noon, found Seth Woodlow slung across his own saddle. Earlier that morning the pair had taken up their vigil from the tree line above the Svensson ranch and had been rewarded when the girl on her pinto had quit the place at a gallop. Covering the options that she was either going to a rendezvous with her brother or acting as a decoy for some activity at the ranch, they separated. Seth set off in pursuit of Jenny while Hank remained hidden, watching for a visit from the kid or the departure of the father for some secret meeting place. By mid-morning, weary of inactivity and certain that the Swede was occupied with the everyday tasks on a horse ranch, he mounted up and set off to follow Seth's trail.

Jenny Svensson's reputation with horses was common knowledge in Tatanka Crossing, as indeed was the fact that she could be seen exercising several of them each day on the rangeland around her home. But she'd been gone for more than three hours; too long, in Hank's opinion, for an exercise run, thus prompting the thought that she had gone to meet her brother.

With luck, he thought, Seth would have followed her to his lair and the kid's capture would be attributed to their vigilance. Brent Deacon had been angry that the kid had got away the night they'd killed Jed Prescott, but if they completed the job now there might be some financial reward. It was a slim hope, but, for him, it would be no hope at all if Seth did the job alone. So he spurred his horse on, anxious to catch up with his partner and share the anticipated spoils.

Hank spotted Seth's horse half a mile across the grassland when he was still three miles from the river. The horse was attempting to graze but every minute or so would jerk into a trot for half a dozen paces before lowering its head to the ground again. As he approached, Hank could hear the sound of Seth's voice, his cursing growing louder and more desperate the closer he drew. When Seth heard the approaching rider he ceased yelling, waited for him to circle around his horse so that he could identify him.

'What happened to you?' Hank asked as he cut Seth free from the rope.

Seth's explanation was brief, his concern more centred on what they did next. 'I'm for leaving the territory,' he told Hank. 'This Charlie Jefferson will kill us if he catches us near the Svensson place and until the kid is caught that is exactly what Deacon will expect of us. What do you say, Hank? We can drift down to Kansas. Perhaps hire on as trail hands? Or head for Texas. There'll be herds heading north before winter.'

Hank was less interested in moving on. Pushing cattle was hard, dusty work. He'd grown accustomed to hanging around the Last Dollar, pushing nothing heavier than cards and coins around a table. Besides, Charlie Jefferson had got the best of him once; he owed him for the beating he'd taken and was reluctant to leave town until that debt had been paid. Perhaps he couldn't take him on his own

101

but the two of them could waylay him, wreak such revenge on him that he would never bother them again.

He was in the middle of this explanation when he spotted the distant rider. Hatless, hair flowing freely in her wake, Jenny on her pinto was as easy to recognize as a buffalo in a herd of sheep. 'She's alone,' he said. 'I thought Jefferson was with her.'

Seth stated the obvious. 'They must have parted.'

'Where has she been? Coming down from the hills! Earlier she was at Bull Creek.'

'Her brother,' said Hank. 'He must be somewhere up there.'

'What'll we do?' Seth's question was asked nervously. He didn't want to do anything except gather up his belongings from his room in Tatanka Crossing and head for the nearest border.

'We could have a ride up there. Perhaps we'll spot him, or at least find his hideout.' Hank thought for a moment. 'On the other hand, someone with local knowledge might be able to suggest a likely place. Come on. Let's get back to town and report to Gus Tarleton or Deacon.'

'Then we'll ride clear away,' Seth muttered low, but Hank was already in the saddle and heading back towards Tatanka Crossing.

By coincidence, Hank and Seth arrived back in Tatanka Crossing at the same time as Gus Tarleton, they coming from the west and he, having crossed the bridge from the south bank of the Tatanka, from the east. By noon it had become clear to Gus that Brent Deacon had been wrong in his assessment that Charlie Jefferson was travelling to Laramie or, if he had, he had chosen a different route from that which passed by Horn Hill. Eventually, bored with dealing out solitaire and hungry because he'd been at his station since first light, he'd rinsed the muggy taste of his black cigarillos from his mouth with a first gulp of water which he then spat into the dirt, and swallowed a second to clear his throat.

He didn't rush back to Tatanka Crossing. Brent Deacon, he knew, would be angry that he hadn't accomplished his task. Not that he was afraid of Deacon, but he didn't like the man's attempts to treat him like one of the incompetent rannies he kept around to answer his beck and call. He, Gus Tarleton, was better than that and, if it became necessary, he would prove it to Deacon just as he would prove it to Charlie Jefferson the first time he got him in his gun sights.

Brent Deacon had been anxious for news all morning, couldn't understand why Gus Tarleton hadn't yet returned to town, so he was at the window of the bank when the tall gunman rode into town. Deacon went outside to meet him, by which time Hank and Seth had dismounted and hitched their horses to the rail.

'Is it done?' Deacon directed his question at Gus Tarleton.

Gus shook his head. 'Never showed.'

Disbelief was evident in Deacon's expression, an accusation that Tarleton had, in some way, been tardy in his performance forming on his lips. Gus forestalled him, told him he'd been at Horn Hill before the sun. 'Jefferson didn't go that way.'

'Jefferson?' It was Seth who spoke. 'Charlie Jefferson?' he asked for confirmation. 'He was with the Svensson girl west a-way along the river this morning.'

'You saw him?'

'I followed the girl. They met up. Looked like an arranged meeting. Like they were sparking.'

'And you didn't kill him?' hissed Deacon.

103

Although he'd agreed with Hank to say nothing about the incident that had led to him being tied to his horse, Seth was still unwilling to let such criticism go undefended. 'I was doing what I was told to do,' he argued. 'Trailing the girl. Hoping she would lead us to her brother.'

'And did she?' Deacon's tone made it evident that he expected a negative answer.

It was Hank who responded. 'Yeah. We think he's up in the northern hills.' He gave his reasons for the speculation. 'We figured that someone with local knowledge would know if there were any likely places the kid could use for a hideout.'

Aggrieved at Gus Tarleton's failure to prevent Charlie Jefferson reaching Laramie, Brent Deacon was only mildly appeased by the possibility of catching Lars Svensson and preventing him from disclosing anything he might have learned from Jed Prescott. Then Hank spoke again. 'Perhaps Jefferson didn't go to Laramie. Perhaps he's with the kid.'

Deacon's first reaction was to dismiss the suggestion but the longer it played in his mind the more he convinced himself that it was a possibility. Charlie Jefferson appeared intent on involving himself in the affairs of the valley and where better to start if, as Seth Woodlow hinted, there was something between him and the Svensson girl? Their meeting this morning could have been a precursor to meeting her brother and if the girl had returned from that meeting alone it was quite possible that Charlie Jefferson had remained with him. After all, his father still had a few days in which to come up with the money. If Charlie Jefferson hadn't gone to Laramie this morning then tomorrow or the next day would do just as well.

'I know someone who might have the information

we're seeking,' he said. 'Wait for me in the Last Dollar. Time I paid a visit to my wounded brother-in-law.'

With the position of the old trapper's shack fixed in their heads, along with the instruction to kill anyone and everyone found there, Gus Tarleton, Hank Swales and a reluctant Seth Woodlow rode north from Tatanka Crossing. Zach Prescott had described the vicinity of the shack to Brent Deacon, and had warned that, in daylight, anyone approaching would be clear targets as soon as they were within rifle range. Accordingly, the three men waited for the cover of darkness before making their move, advancing on the old timber building from three sides.

The lack of activity while awaiting the shield of night had prepared them for an empty hideout, nonetheless they approached with stealth, guns ready, and fired rounds into the darkness of the single room when they burst through the door. There was no one there, but when they lit the candles that had been left on the flimsy table they discovered evidence aplenty that the place had been recently used. They had missed their quarry by a day, a fact which would not mollify Brent Deacon.

CHAPTER TWELVE

Next morning, bad news for Brent Deacon was threefold and for the first time since arriving in Tatanka Crossing he sensed that he wasn't in complete control of events. The first indication that the day would not go well was as he walked along Main Street from his home to his office in the Last Dollar. Passing Kincaid's Eating Parlour he saw Gus Tarleton and the others eating breakfast. It was clear from their sombre demeanour, their apparent lack of interest in each other and in the food on their plates that their mission in the northern hills had ended in failure. Hank Swales watched the banker pass by before informing Gus. The tall gunfighter rose without a word and went outside. He caught up to Deacon as he reached the board-walk on the far side of the street, outside the bank building. In a low voice he apprised his boss of their findings in the northern hills.

'Nobody there,' he said, 'but that's where the kid has been hiding out.'

Brent Deacon shrugged off the disappointment; he wasn't unduly surprised. He'd been hopeful of catching Lars Svensson there, but the chances of catching Charlie Jefferson, who was currently his major concern, had been nothing but a long shot, at best.

'Do you think he's still using the place? Will he go back there?'

'Your guess is as good as mine,' said Tarleton. 'There was nothing to say he would and nothing to say he wouldn't. Do you want us to keep an eye on the place?'

Deacon shook his head. He figured it might warrant another visit tonight but he would decide that later. 'I'll send for you when I want you,' he told Tarleton, then went on down the street to the Last Dollar.

The swamper muttered a gruff greeting, then handed over a vellum envelope which Deacon instantly recognized.

'Came in on the stage last night,' the swamper told him. Deacon grunted a response and carried the letter through to the back office.

The letter was from Cincinnati Enterprises and the tenor of its contents was more curt, more severe than any previous correspondence. The last letter, a month earlier, had carried a hint of impatience because of the lack of progress, but this went much further. Word had reached them that a rival mining company was seeking sanction to survey the area. Unlike Cincinnati Enterprises, whose surveys had been clandestine, they would undoubtedly reveal their findings and the price of land would rise accordingly. It was essential that the valley belonged to Cincinnati Enterprises before the end of summer.

The final paragraph made it clear that if Brent had not completed the purchase of at least part of the valley by the end of the current month then his position with the company was in jeopardy.

Wordlessly, he extracted the Cincinnati Enterprise file from a cupboard and placed the letter inside. He studied the file for a moment; recollected that this was the one he had left open on his desk; the one Jed Prescott had seen and had understood immediately the relevance of its contents.

Though at first it had seemed an error of judgement to leave the correspondence unattended, Brent now realized that the train of events that had followed had become an advantage to the fulfilment of his plans. Killing Jed Prescott had been essential. He couldn't be permitted to spread the information he'd gleaned; not the fact that Brent wanted the land for Cincinnati Enterprises, nor that the valley was rich in copper and silver deposits.

In Brent's opinion, cattlemen, who only judged land by the quality of its grass, were not being cheated if they were given a good market price for grazing land. After all, they had no reason to suppose that the purchaser had any other use for it, and in this instance they would never know they were selling to Cincinnati Enterprises. He, on the other hand, did know and when he had control of the Prescott land, which he intended would be some time soon, he would demand top dollar for it from his employers.

Of course, killing Jed Prescott had had another benefit. Branding Lars Svensson as his slayer served not only to drive a wedge between the Prescott and Svensson families but, by applying proper pressure, could result in the Swedish horse rancher being driven out of the valley. Applying pressure was Brent Deacon's strong point, as Taub Svensson would discover as soon as Dagg Jefferson's ranch had been swallowed up by the bank. It was a thought that caused Brent Deacon to smile. His own cleverness was a constant source of pleasure to him. The two setbacks of the morning were nothing more than that, he thought. By the end of the month, when the bank had repossessed the Jeffersons' land, the other landowner, Tommy Humboldt, would bow to the inevitable and sell up. When Charlie Jefferson and Lars Svensson were removed from the scene there would be no obstacle to the completion of his plans.

Invigorated by these thoughts of success, Brent Deacon stepped outside the Last Dollar, on to the boardwalk to watch the bustle of the day develop: the traders preparing their premises; the townswomen shopping; the lad from the telegraph office running along the street, flimsy paper in hand, carrying a message of some urgency for someone. It was a matter of interest to Brent Deacon that that someone happened to be Sheriff Simms. Seconds later the boy emerged and made his way back to the telegraph office at a much more leisurely pace.

Two minutes later, Tom Simms left his office, looked up and down the street and, catching sight of Brent Deacon, crossed the street.

'Good morning, Sheriff.'

Tom Simms removed his hat and rubbed a red bandanna around the inside rim before delivering Deacon's third piece of bad news.

'You'll have to withdraw that reward for the Svensson boy.' Brent gave the sheriff a quizzical look but said nothing. 'Got a telegram from Jim Tozer, the marshal down in Laramie. The kid turned up there yesterday claiming to be innocent of murder and demanding that the marshal comes here to investigate and find the real killer.'

'What will he do?'

'He'll come here, that's what he'll do.' Tom Simms spoke angrily, like a man who'd been let down by those around him. 'Wants to know why he hasn't been informed about the killing, especially when it's a Prescott who's dead.'

'Is it his business?'

109

'It is when a posse is organized. I told you that when you were organizing your boys to go after the kid. My jurisdiction begins and ends in this town I don't have the authority to arrest people anywhere else.'

'So the kid's in jail in Laramie?'

'Not necessarily. Depends what he's told the marshal and what the marshal believes. Without a formal charge from me he has no reason to arrest him.'

'Then send one off,' snapped Brent, then immediately he changed his mind. 'No. No, leave it. Let us wait until the marshal gets here. See what his attitude is. The situation might be resolved by that time.' Sheriff Simms gave him an anxious look. 'Quit worrying,' Deacon added before going back inside the Last Dollar.

He'd told the sheriff not to worry but Brent Deacon was doing exactly that. Perhaps, before he was shot, Jed Prescott had passed on some information to Lars Svensson, and if he had, then depending on what he knew, disclosure could ruin the plans he had for the Tatanka valley. Also, an investigation by a federal marshal might persuade some townspeople to speak in favour of the kid. So far, no one had spoken out in his defence, but those who sat in the Last Dollar each night, cowed by Gus Tarleton's guns, were apt to be braver when questioned by a frontier marshal. Lars Svensson had to be silenced for good and Deacon believed he knew a man who could do it. He sent for Hank Swales.

'I want you to go to Laramie,' Deacon told him. 'Find a man called Lou Greene. Point out the Svensson kid to him and tell him there's five hundred dollars if he never leaves there. Get it done quickly and save the marshal a journey. And keep a lookout for Jefferson. Don't let him see you either on the trail or in Laramie.'

Hank was tired. He'd had no sleep for twenty-four

110

hours but he knew better than to offer that as an excuse for delaying his departure. Instead, he went straight to the livery stable and saddled his pony. Seth Woodlow was sitting on the porch out front of the Last Dollar when Hank came down the street. He stood and Hank reined in beside him.

'Where are you going?' asked Seth.

'Got a job to do for Deacon. Won't be back until tomorrow.' He rode on heading for the bridge to take him across the Tatanka.

Beyond the Feather Waters, where Horn Hill towered away to his right and the trail to Laramie veered away to his left, Hank dismounted. It was cool here, high trees providing shade from the sun at its zenith. He was tired and despite Brent Deacon's orders he needed to sleep. The time of his arrival at Laramie was of little matter. Deacon's instructions implied that the kid wouldn't be leaving there any time soon, so he lay down, tipped his hat over his eyes and settled himself for the satisfaction of three hours' sleep. In the event, it was a little longer than that and might have been longer still but for an unlikely disturbance.

Charlie Jefferson left Laramie with $12,000 in his saddlebags and a fury in his breast which he knew would best be assuaged by putting his fist in Brent Deacon's face. His anger had been aroused by a visit to the military encampment where he'd spoken to the commanding officer. Colonel MacDonald had apprised him of the situation regarding the purchase of cattle from the Tatanka valley. This year the army had, in fact, purchased more cattle from that source, not fewer, and the stockyard was still full with the last supply that had been driven to Laramie three weeks earlier. When Charlie checked them out he saw that

111

they all had the Circle P brand burned into their hide.

From the fort Charlie had returned to the town, collected his money from the bank, then stopped off at the hotel to have a parting word with Lars Svensson. Once again, Charlie was struck by the lad's facial resemblance to his sister, but while he thought of Jenny as a young woman, he understood why everyone still referred to her brother as the kid. At that moment a petulant look spoke wordlessly of his reluctance to stay alone in Laramie.

'We'll get you home as soon as possible, Lars, but in the meantime it's safer for you here. The marshal will keep an eye on you.' They'd parted on the porch of the Laramie House Hotel.

Charlie was three miles out of Laramie when he became aware that he was being followed. Conscious of the money he was carrying and that anyone in the bank that morning would have seen the large withdrawal, he readied himself for robbers. At the first appropriate spot, he pulled off the trail, eased his gun from its holster and waited. Several minutes later a lone rider passed the copse in which Charlie hid. The horse was a black-and-white pinto, the rider Lars Svensson.

'The marshal sent a telegraph message to Sheriff Simms telling him I was in Laramie,' Lars explained. 'I figured if everyone in Tatanka Crossing thinks I'm in Laramie then the safest place for me is back home.'

Charlie had reservations about such logic but he chose not to argue. The boy was old enough to make his own decisions.

'You can't go home,' was all he said, 'you can stay with my folks until this is sorted out.'

The heat of the morning restricted them to a casual pace. Little was said until they saw the shape of Horn Hill ahead.

112

'Once across the Feather Waters we'll cut east again, go around the town until we're on Jefferson land. Nobody will see us,' advised Charlie.

Lars had dropped back a couple of paces, was looking down at the pinto's rear right leg as if it had a limp.

'Hey Charlie,' he called, 'my sis, she likes you.' The words came out strangely, as though he couldn't decide if he was asking a question or making a statement.

'Why shouldn't she?' Charlie asked.

'No reason,' Lars responded. He'd had the feeling he spoken out of turn. It worried him that he might have offended Charlie Jefferson. He didn't see the grin on Charlie's face, nor the fact that it took on a serious expression as he looked ahead towards Horn Hill.

After Hank had ridden away, Seth walked along to the rooming-house and lay on his bed. Like Hank, he was in need of sleep and it came to him within minutes of lying down. He woke three hours later with a troubled mind and a sore jaw where Charlie Jefferson had hit him. The thought of tangling with Jefferson again worried him but, if he stayed on in Tatanka Crossing and took more orders from Brent Deacon, that was exactly what would happen. He'd tried to persuade Hank to move on but he'd been unwilling to agree. They'd been partners for four years but Seth decided that now was the time for the parting of the ways. He'd rather be eating trail dust than Charlie Jefferson's fist or, worse yet, his lead. Seth packed his saddle-bags and left the rooming house.

Seth had no definite plan when he left Tatanka Crossing other than to get away without being seen by Gus Tarleton or Brent Deacon. By using the rear doors to leave the livery stable, riding around the back of Main Street and fording the Tatanka well east of the settlement, he achieved that aim. He didn't ride fast, figuring that if he reached Laramie by nightfall he could make an early start next day, which would get him far from Tatanka Crossing. Texas as a destination loomed large in his mind. A big country, Texas. A man could lose himself there.

He'd crossed the Feather Waters, climbed the ridge with Horn Hill to his right and the trail to Laramie dropping away to his left, when he spotted the two approaching riders. Seth had always been a cautious traveller; his natural reaction was to pause among the trees to avoid the horsemen, but at this moment an inexplicable fear clutched him, as though those approaching were war-painted warriors searching the plains specifically for him. He watched and as they came closer he recognized both men.

A cold sweat beaded his brow. He dismounted, meaning to smuggle himself deeper among the trees to prevent them from seeing him. As he stepped down and drew the reins over his mount's head his gaze rested on the stock of the rifle sticking out of the saddle boot. The thought of vengeance against Charlie Jefferson played in his imagination, together with the reward that had been offered for the Svensson kid. He rubbed his hand across his mouth. Touched the rifle. Withdrew it and walked stealthily towards a forked tree which would provide a steady resting place for the rifle.

The riders were closing, not travelling fast. Charlie Jefferson was riding in front but was turned in the saddle apparently talking to Lars Svensson on the pinto behind. Seth sighted along the barrel. Vengeance won out over reward, or perhaps it was fear. If he hit only one he didn't want Charlie Jefferson seeking his own revenge. He squinted and his finger rested on the trigger.

At that moment a voice broke the silence. 'Hey, Seth.

114

What are you doing?'

Hank's call startled more than Seth. His horse snorted and threw its head, and two pigeons flew up and away from the tree in which they had silently awaited the breaking of the tension that Seth had created. Seth turned his head towards Hank; his eyes were large, his lips drawn back almost in a snarl. Then he turned his attention once again to his target and squeezed the trigger. It was a hurried shot and Seth cursed as he fired because he knew he hadn't hit Charlie Jefferson.

If tracking rebel fugitives had taught Charlie anything, it was the telltale signs of ambush. First among those was the startled movement of wildlife, and the sudden rising of the two birds alerted him immediately. Instantly, his keen eyesight caught movement behind the lower foliage and the kind of fleeting glint that is produced by sunlight on metal. Even so, had Seth taken an instant longer, an instant to ensure he would hit his target, Charlie would never have heard the zing nor felt the air movement of the passing bullet. He fell from his horse, a reflex action to give the shooter a smaller target at which to aim, but as he fell he heard a yell from behind and knew that Lars had been hit.

Another shot rang out, the aim more wild than the first, for Charlie neither saw nor felt any effect of the bullet. He wheeled his horse so that it was side on to the shooter, providing more protection while he scurried to where Lars lay. The boy's face was white and twisted in a grimace of pain. There was blood on his shirt, spreading from a hole just above his waist on his right side. The gunman fired again. His intention seemed to be to scatter the horses but Charlie was holding tight to the lead rein of his own, and the pinto, while nervy, seemed reluctant to go anywhere without Lars.

A small depression in the ground was the only cover available, so, still holding the animal's lead rein, Charlie got his hands under the wounded lad's arms and dragged him to its relative safety. It was during this operation that Charlie assessed that there were two gunmen, spotting the small whiffs of smoke among the trees as he scuttled Lars into the depression.

Although the hole they occupied offered some protection it was at best only temporary. The ambushers had the advantage of high ground where they could wait for Charlie and Lars to make a move. As soon as they did they would be open targets and easily picked off. It was clear to Charlie that he and Lars couldn't remain where they were. Lars was wounded, in pain and in need of medical treatment. He scanned the area, seeking an escape route but they were still pretty much on open scrubland. Eventually, off to the left, Charlie spotted the only feature in the terrain that gave him any hope of a way out. It was a slim hope but the only one.

A fold of land, a ridge which grew deeper the higher it climbed, was evident some fifty yards away. From the base of the hillside it apparently ran clear to the top, certainly higher than the gunmen were positioned. If he could reach it without getting shot it gave him a means of getting behind the ambushers and turning the tables. It wouldn't be easy. Perhaps they would see him, anticipate his plan and catch him like a rat in a trap, but there was no alternative.

'Are you able to use a gun?' he asked Lars.

'I haven't got one,' Lars said. 'Only the rifle which is with my horse.'

The pinto had moved a dozen yards, close enough to conjure up thoughts of trying to reach it, but too far in reality for Charlie to make it without being shot in the process.

116

'What do you want,' he asked. 'Pistol or rifle?'

Charlie's plan was for Lars to provide some covering fire while he made a dash for the ridge. The range of the rifle would achieve that more effectively but, considering the wound he'd sustained, a pistol might be easier for Lars to handle. That was what he chose. Charlie gave Lars his pistol and dropped some extra shells on to the ground beside him. He pulled his horse close to him and dragged the rifle from its scabbard, clutched the front and back of the saddle and said, 'Now.'

Lars raised his head, fired twice, then sank down as a wave of pain swept over him. Clinging to one side of his horse, Indian style, Charlie directed it towards the high ground. He hoped the gunmen couldn't see him, hoped they thought the gunfire had spooked his mount. The guns from the tree line started again. Charlie didn't know whether any of the shots were aimed in his direction. He kept the horse running, could see the deepening fault line and when he considered that the ridge was high enough to hide him he dropped and rolled, rifle gripped tight in his hand.

The horse ran on a few yards but came to a halt when it reached the trees. Charlie slithered forward until the ridge line was high enough for him to make progress at a crouch. From the sound of the hillside gunfire he esti-mated he was still a distance below the gunmen's position but, in case they had seen his manoeuvre, in case one of the gunmen was watching for his emergence from the ridge, he forsook the naturally formed pathway.

Using the cover of bushes and trees he moved diago-nally up and away from the estimated position of his opponents. Guided by the sound of gunfire he halted when he knew himself to be holding the highest ground. The gunfire was sporadic and little of it, if any, was coming

117

from the bottom of the hill. He hoped that Lars had not been hit again.

He saw their horses first, low-necked cow ponies with thin, untidy manes that looked black against chestnut bodies. They both turned their heads in his direction, big, black eyes observing as he stepped clear of high shrubbery, his rifle in both hands, poised to sweep it in any direction from which danger threatened. One horse snickered, a low, friendly sound, as though appreciative of the warm day, lush grass and shady arbour in which he had been tethered. It was a tranquil moment, out of place with the violence that had brought Charlie to this spot, but it was shattered by another gunshot. Although muffled by the surrounding trees, the report was clear enough for Charlie to know that the gunmen had advanced downhill.

Concerned for Lars Svensson's safety he stepped forward quickly, almost too quickly, almost without observing that level of caution that had served him well during the war and for those dangerous years immediately after. But his instinct for survival hadn't deserted him. Perhaps it was a movement captured in the periphery of his sight, or perhaps it was the rustle of leaves or grass, but something warned him of a presence to his right.

He threw himself forward, twisting, pulling the trigger of his Winchester even as he recognized the red shirt of Hank Swales. Flame burst from Hank's rifle at the same moment as Charlie's, but his shot went high over Charlie's plunging form, while Charlie's bullet struck Hank in the midriff, punching him backwards, doubling him over, causing him to drop his rifle so that he could clutch at the pain where his body had been punctured. He knew nothing about Charlie's second shot. It hit him in the chest, knocked him off his feet and he was dead before he hit the ground.

118

Charlie stood, took a step towards his victim but then a voice called from further down the hill, reminding him that the job wasn't completed.

'Hank! Hank!' The call was tentative, nervous, unsure. When Charlie stepped from the cover of the tree line he saw Seth midway to the spot where Lars lay. Seth's eyes widened with surprise and fear. Without hesitation he threw aside his weapon. 'Don't shoot,' he pleaded. 'Don't shoot.'

'Why not?' asked Charlie. 'I told you to stay away from the Svensson family. If Lars is dead then so are you.'

'No, please,' pleaded Seth. 'I'll tell you anything you want to know. Hank killed Jed Prescott,' he blurted.

Charlie glared at him, disgust mingled with his dislike, but a witness who would clear Lars of murder was too valuable to destroy.

'Keep it for the sheriff,' he said, then drove the butt of his rifle into Seth's stomach, rendering him incapable of resistance. Tending to Lars Svensson's wound was Charlie's first priority.

The bullet had gone straight through Lars Svensson. The positions of the holes, front and back, suggested it had missed all of his vital organs. However, loss of blood and the risk of blood poisoning still presented a serious threat to his life. Charlie worked quickly, ripping the sleeves from his own shirt to use as wadding in the wound holes, securing them in place with a belt that he took from the dead Hank Swales.

Lars was conscious but weak when they set off again. Aware that the lad was likely to pass out on the journey, Charlie shared his horse, sitting behind the saddle on the pinto to ensure that Lars didn't fall. They travelled slowly and presented an odd party when they came in sight of the Jefferson ranch house. Seth Woodlow, bound but upright,

119

led the way followed by Charlie and Lars on the pinto, behind which came the riderless roan with a body slung over the saddle of the trailing cow pony.

Lars became a nursing cause for his mother and she ordered a couple of their farmhands to carry the wounded lad into the house. At Charlie's insistence, his father saddled a horse and rode with him to Tatanka Crossing. Charlie wanted his father to have the satisfaction of dropping the $12,000 on to Brent Deacon's desk.

CHAPTER THIRTEEN

One of Tommy Humboldt's crew, higher up the approach trail to Tatanka Crossing, had looked back and seen the quartet of horses in his wake; so by the time Charlie Jefferson and Dagg reached the settlement with the bound Seth Woodlow riding in front and the horse bearing Hank Swales's corpse tagging along behind, word of their approach had already spread along Main Street. Heads turned to watch their passing. Others, more curious, accompanied their progress, some matching their pace along the boardwalk and others following behind in the dust. One fellow, more determined than the other townspeople, lifted the head of the body slung over the rear horse.

'Hank Swales,' he declared, but given Seth Woodlow's sorry predicament on the lead horse, the announcement took nobody by surprise.

Questions were asked among those gathering around the group but none was openly addressed to Charlie or his father. They remained silent until they were in front of the sheriff's office, where Tom Simms waited. His hands clasped both edges of his open waistcoat, tugging it straight so that the badge on the left side faced in the direction of the approaching party, making his authority in the town clear for all to see. Brad Keen, his deputy, lounged in habitual fashion against a porch post to the sheriff's right.

'Do you want to explain what's going on here?' asked Tom Simms.

'I was bushwhacked by these two over by Horn Hill,' explained Charlie. 'It didn't turn out the way they planned.'

Sheriff Simms turned his attention to Seth Woodlow. 'Is this true?'

'It was Hank's idea,' said the prisoner, eager to shift the blame for all their wrongdoings on to his dead partner. There were murmurs and nods among the crowd. No-one had any doubt that Hank Swales and Seth Woodlow were capable of ambush and, given their recent history with Charlie Jefferson, an act of revenge was not unexpected.

'Step down,' the sheriff told Seth.

'You've got something else to say first,' said Charlie.

Seth licked his lips. His glance darted from place to place, hoping to find a reason to stay silent, but when Charlie prompted him again, he repeated the statement he'd made earlier.

'Jed Prescott wasn't killed by the Svensson kid. Hank did it. He pulled the trigger.'

Once again there were comments from the crowd but it was Sheriff Simms's voice that carried above the hubbub. 'Why did he do it?'

'We were paid to.' It was unclear whether Seth realized he'd admitted to playing a part in Jed Prescott's death because, once begun, he now seemed determined to reveal all he knew. 'Jed had some information about—'

At that moment a shot rang out, striking Seth in the back of the head, pitching him from the back of his horse to form a bloody bundle on the street. Another shot rang out. Fortunately for Charlie he had, at the moment of the first shot, begun to dismount and, in continuing to do so, managed to avoid the bullet that was intended to do to him what the previous one had done to his prisoner.

The crowd scattered. Horses, startled by the bullets and the reaction of the people around, reared and stomped, tried to pull away from the poles to which they were fastened.

'Top window,' Charlie heard someone shout, then he discovered it was Brad Keen who, with drawn pistol, was heading across the street to the Last Dollar. Charlie looked up at the building. The corner window was open; a flimsy yellow curtain, sucked outside by the breeze, flapped like a cavalry pennant at the charge. Whoever had been in that room had now gone, but evidence of their presence lingered. A telltale trace of blue gunsmoke hovered outside the window.

Charlie caught up with the deputy. 'I'll go inside,' he insisted. 'You go round the back. Block off that route. Stop anybody who tries to leave.'

Brad Keen looked ready to debate the deployment, ready to argue that his position as deputy sheriff made it his responsibility to go in through the front batwings, but Charlie Jefferson had already moved ahead, had already gained the porch which, moments earlier, had been crowded with interested onlookers but where now only two or three remained, anxiously clustered at the furthest end, well away from windows and door.

Cautiously, Charlie approached the doorway from the side, chancing a look around the frame, only a portion of his face showing to those inside. A bullet smashed against the timber above his head, then another. Charlie withdrew but his retreat was only momentary. He dived forward, under the batwings, and sprawled on the floor of the Last

Dollar, right arm extended, revolver gripped tightly, hammer held back in readiness for a quick shot.

There was movement inside the room but no more shots. Chairs scraped across the floor, a table overturned and a door banged shut as men and women sought refuge from the expected gunfight. Those who had never left the saloon, those who had shown little interest in Charlie's arrival in town or had been more excited by affairs at the gaming tables or the company of friends or dancehall girls, now looked to find a corner safe from flying lead. Those shots from above which had led to the death of Seth Woodlow had alerted the occupants of the room below to the developing situation, but not until shots had been fired across the saloon had the nearness of their own death or injury been an issue. Now they pushed, stumbled and hurried to the rear of the room, careful not to look at Charlie Jefferson lest he saw something in their expression that would mark them as his enemy.

When it became apparent to Charlie that whoever had fired at him was no longer in the room, he got to his feet. Judging by the position of everyone else it was clear that a pathway had been cleared for him to the door to the back office. He remembered the sound of the banging door as he'd hit the floor. He cast a last look at those congregated against the back wall; then, assured that they were no threat to him, advanced on it. He pressed himself against the wall at one side of the door and yelled so that whoever was in the next room would hear him.

'This is Charlie Jefferson. Come out with your hands up.'

There was silence. No response. Then gunshots, which came not from the next room but beyond that, from outside the building. Charlie opened the door. The room was empty but the door to the rear alley stood ajar.

'It's Charlie Jefferson,' he shouted again to make sure that Deputy Keen didn't open fire on him when he stepped outside. But the chances of that were non-existent. Brad Keen lay on his back, arms spread wide and gave only the slightest movement of his legs, an involuntary spasm as death settled on him.

Charlie rushed to him and raised his head. Blood dribbled from Brad's mouth as he tried to speak. Charlie bent a little closer, struggling to hear the dying deputy's words.

'Gus Tarleton,' he said. He stared up into Charlie's face with a strange expression of surprise, repeated his message, 'Gus Tarleton,' then died.

By this time Sheriff Simms and a couple of townsmen had reached the scene. 'Gus Tarleton,' Charlie declared.

Sheriff Simms nodded. 'We saw him. He went down there.' Simms pointed to an alley that branched off to the right. Charlie went off in the direction indicated while the sheriff attended to his dead deputy.

The alley that Charlie followed worked its way in a westerly direction. It separated the back yards of some private homes from the rear entrances of some Main Street buildings. Charlie moved forward cautiously, not knowing if Gus Tarleton had a specific destination or if he was trying to get as far ahead of any pursuers as it was possible to get.

It was a couple of moments before Charlie realized that the livery stable was the end building. Up ahead he could hear the mild commotion of the animals that were in the outside corral. Figuring it was Tarleton's plan to reach his horse and then ride clear of Tatanka Crossing almost caused Charlie to miss his quarry.

Tarleton was in shadow, trying to gain entrance to one of the buildings, working a door-handle with growing impatience until the truth became apparent to him. A door he had expected to be open was locked. He'd been left to fend for himself. In frustration he slammed his fist against the door. It was that action that caught Charlie's attention. At the same moment, Tarleton turned and saw Charlie. With the desperation of a hunted man he fired his rifle, once, twice, thrice, the bullets smacking into the wall near Charlie, pressing him into a doorway, needing its protection to avoid the bullets that sped his way. While he was making use of this shelter, Gus Tarleton broke from cover and ran along the alley.

Charlie fired two shots at the fleeing figure but neither did any damage. At the first opportunity he began his pursuit. Gus Tarleton was well ahead and making a direct line for the horses. Charlie followed, sparing a glance at the building to which Gus had tried to gain access. It was the bank. Charlie didn't think it was coincidence that Gus had chosen that door.

Progressing carefully, Charlie reached the end of the alley. He paused, peered round the corner. There were several horses in the corral, the rigs for most of them, saddle, bridle and blanket, slung over the top rail. They seemed restless, shuffling around as if they'd caught the whiff of a distant bear. There was no sign of Gus Tarleton. Charlie guessed he was inside the stable, preparing his own horse for departure.

Quietly, crossing the space between the end of the alley and the livery stable door, Charlie moved in a crouched run. He peered around the door into the darkness of the stable. It was a long, timber-built building redolent with the smell of horses and leather. Charlie counted eight stalls, above which was a loft brimful of hay.

Charlie stepped inside, waited a moment to let his eyes become accustomed to the lack of light. Passively, the horses in the stalls watched him, unconcerned by his pres-ence. Still, Charlie was cautious. Gus Tarleton had to be

126

around somewhere. There was no stableman on the premises. Charlie wondered what had happened to him. It was unusual for a livery to be unattended.

He looked up at the loft, checked for movement up there, or falling straw. Nothing. He began to make his way through the stable, the double doors at the front were open. Perhaps Tarleton had gone straight through. Coming here could have been a ruse. His horse could be saddled and waiting elsewhere.

He checked each stall, aware that any of them could be Tarleton's refuge and, if so, that he presented an easy target for the gunman. He had almost reached the last one when a man in dungarees and old sweat-stained hat entered. For a moment they regarded each other with suspicion.

'You the stableman?' Charlie asked.

'That's me.'

'Anyone come through here in the last few minutes?'

'Nope. Been out front all the time. Some excitement up the street.'

'Two men have been killed,' Charlie informed him. 'Gus Tarleton killed them. I think he came here for his horse.'

'Tarleton.' The man's voice was raspy, as though he wanted to spit. He didn't. 'Tarleton's horse is out there in the corral.'

Quickly, Charlie backtracked through the stable. There was a loud neigh from a horse out in the corral. Charlie stepped outside, casting an eye over the horses within the poles. At first he noticed nothing different. The horses were milling around but not fretting. He wondered which one belonged to Gus Tarleton.

Then he saw it in the middle of the herd. The big chestnut had been saddled and was being steered towards the

127

gate. Tarleton was in among the horse, keeping low, hoping to gain an advantage over Charlie.

'It's no good, Tarleton,' Charlie shouted. 'You can't escape.'

Tarleton's answer was to shoot at Charlie. He was using his revolver now because, once he was mounted, it would be an easier weapon to handle. The bullet sang away beyond Charlie, who watched as Tarleton climbed into the saddle and fired another shot in Charlie's direction. The other horses in the corral were becoming nervous, swinging away from where Tarleton sat astride his chestnut gelding.

Seeing his opportunity, Gus set spur to horse and urged it forward. Charlie realized that Gus's intention was not to open the gate but to jump the poles. Grabbing a blanket from the rail he ran to intercept them. Gus fired. The bullet kicked up dirt behind Charlie. A second shot was no closer. By now Gus needed to concentrate on clearing the fence. While man and horse were in the air Charlie positioned himself close to where they would touch down.

Frantically waving the blanket, Charlie distracted the horse. It stumbled and pitched Gus forward over its head. Instantly he was on his feet and running. He turned to fire another shot at Charlie but a voice from the alley caused him to change his aim.

'Tarleton,' yelled Sheriff Simms. Gus brought his weapon to bear on the law officer but Tom Simms shot first. The first shot hit Tarleton in the chest and was probably lethal but the sheriff fired again to be certain.

Sheriff Simms and Charlie stood over the body. 'He was a hired gun,' said Charlie. 'If we'd taken him alive he might have given up some evidence to use against his boss.'

'He killed my deputy,' said Simms. 'That's all the evidence I needed to kill him.'

CHAPTER FOURTEEN

Brent Deacon had been in the Last Dollar when news of Charlie Jefferson's imminent entry into town with Seth Woodlow as his prisoner had been broadcast. The events of the morning had thrown a cloak of nervousness over him that he had been unable to cast off. This latest news, especially the involvement of Charlie Jefferson, reinforced his growing belief that his plans were beginning to crumble and that it was time to move away from Tatanka Crossing.

He drew Gus Tarleton to the end of the bar, away from the other drinkers gathered there. 'Seth's a weak link,' he muttered. 'If he starts to talk to the sheriff he could cause trouble for all of us. Make sure he doesn't.' He cast a look upstairs, a suggestion that one of the bedrooms would provide an ideal vantage point to observe a gathering outside the jail. 'I have some business to take care of at the bank,' he added. 'I'll leave the rear door open. Let yourself in. I'll vouch that you were there with me if you need an alibi.'

Sheriff Simms was leaving his office across the street when Deacon left the Last Dollar but, like most of the people around at that moment, his attention was firmly fixed on the far end of the street. Deacon hurried on, entered the bank which was empty of customers, and greeted the single cashier who was busy with some paperwork behind the counter. Instead of entering his office, Deacon entered the corridor leading to the rear of the building and quietly turned the handle of the outside door. It opened. Just as quietly he closed it again, then turned the key in the lock.

Satisfied that the door was secure he went into his office. Gus Tarleton would only come to the bank if anything went wrong with what he'd been told to do, which would mean that the law was after him. In such circumstances, Brent Deacon wanted nothing to do with him. If he was going to shake off the dust of Tatanka Crossing then he was also going to shake off the likes of Gus Tarleton.

He'd barely sat in the chair behind his desk when the faint report of two rifle shots reached him. He left the office and looked questioningly at the teller. The teller wore an anxious look and his right hand rested on the butt of the revolver he kept under the counter. Outside, people hurried by, running away from the scene of violence. Deacon crossed to the door and opened it.

'What's happening?' he asked the nearest person.

'Somebody shot Seth Woodlow.'

Deacon looked up the street in the direction of the sheriff's office. Men were still congregated there, some on the boardwalk others tending to someone in the dusty street.

'Dead?' asked Deacon.

'Sure is. His partner, too.' Deacon gave him a questioning look. 'Hank Swales,' the man explained. 'Charlie Jefferson brought him in slung over his horse. The two of

131

them tried to bushwhack Charlie.' With that the man moved on, anxious, it seemed, to spread the news to anyone else who hadn't witnessed the shooting.

Brent Deacon cast another look at the activity further up the street. The attention of most people seemed to be focused on the Last Dollar. He could see Tom Simms, gun in hand, issuing instructions, people running here, there and everywhere in response to his bidding. And he saw someone else: Dagg Jefferson, looking in his direction as though he had some reason to accuse him of the violence that had occurred.

More gunfire brought reaction from the people in the street. Men were pointing. Guns were drawn although there didn't seem to be any sense of immediate danger. Quite clearly the shots had not been aimed at them. They came from behind Main Street, from the rear of the Last Dollar if Deacon guessed correctly, which probably meant that Gus Tarleton had been seen, that even now he was heading for the hoped for sanctuary of an open door at the rear of the bank. To establish his innocence of any involvement in the killing of Seth Woodlow, Brent Deacon adopted the expression of a concerned citizen and and walked along the street to where the blood of the unfortunate Woodlow still seeped into the hard-packed earth.

Some minutes later Charlie Jefferson and Sheriff Simms returned to Main Street to announce the death of Gus Tarleton. Publicly, Deacon praised the sheriff for clearing the streets of Tatanka Crossing of a cold-blooded killer. Tom Simms, much to Charlie Jefferson's surprise, seemed genuinely shocked by the killing of his deputy and listened to Deacon with scant regard for his words. Alibi established and public duty done, Deacon returned to the bank.

'I can't see us doing much more business today,' he told

the teller. 'Put the money in the strong room and go home. I have some correspondence to attend to. I'll lock up.'

But five minutes later, before the teller had finished his daily balancing procedure, a customer did arrive at the bank. In fact, there were three men, and when he learned that they were Dagg and Charlie Jefferson and Sheriff Simms it was a worried Brent Deacon who stepped out of his office to meet them.

'Since you saw fit to bring the sheriff when you delivered your ultimatum,' Charlie told him, 'we've brought him to witness the payment of the loan in full.' From his saddle-bags Charlie produced bundles of banknotes. 'We'd like a receipt,' he added.

Deacon's response was different from what had been expected. If, as John Jefferson continually insisted, it was Deacon's intention to ruin his father, then spiking his guns should have been a major disappointment to the banker. Yet Brent Deacon seemed relieved, almost happy to receive the payment, even offering the trio the hospitality of his office and a glass of whiskey to celebrate the conclusion of the transaction. With the money counted and a receipt issued the Jeffersons and Sheriff Simms went on their way.

Brent Deacon had assumed that the visit was the result of some information that Seth Woodlow had passed on to Charlie Jefferson or Sheriff Simms, implicating him in the deaths of Jed Prescott or Sam Flint. He had almost laughed when, instead, Charlie Jefferson had dumped $12,000 on the counter. If his plans had been going well it would have been the last thing he wanted to see, but today, the day when he'd decided to take everything he could get his hands on and quit Tatanka Crossing, it was an unexpected windfall.

133

He would leave under cover of darkness and before leaving he would empty the strongbox at the Last Dollar, the safe at the mercantile, the bank vault and the small wall safe at his home which held Ruth's jewellery in addition to a few hundred dollars in cash. Perhaps the total was a great deal less than he had anticipated with the acquisition of the Prescott land, but at least he'd escape any threat of prison and it would be enough to get him to New Orleans, New York or San Francisco. In a large city he would adopt a new identity, and with sufficient funds would buy his way into a new enterprise which would harvest for him the fortune he craved.

So he spent the remainder of that day doing what was expected of him. He returned home and ate a meal with Ruth. Afterwards, he drove her to Doc Minchin's house to sit with her brother for a while. It was Zach's intention to return next morning to his father's ranch.

While Ruth was visiting her brother Brent went to the Last Dollar. He spent most of the evening in the back office, gathering up the papers that linked him with Cincinnati Enterprises and which he would later destroy somewhere along the route. At the approach of closing time he went home, taking those papers with him but knowing he would have to return when the saloon was in darkness to collect the money from the safe.

Ruth had already returned, the horse and buggy out front attested to that. Brent had assured his wife that he would take care of the stabling when he got home. In fact, he intended using them on the first part of his journey from Tatanka Crossing. The house was in darkness so he assumed his wife to be asleep. He lit a solitary lamp in the parlour and crossed to the wall which housed the safe.

He was loading the contents into a carpetbag when Ruth spoke, her voice surprising him but not startling him

134

in any way or carrying any sort of menace to give him reason to stop.

'What are you doing?'

'Time for me to go,' he said, not turning to look at her.

'Go where?' There was a dawning disquiet in her tone. 'Brent?' she said when he didn't answer.

'Far away,' he told her. 'A big city where no one will ever find me.'

'Those are my jewels,' she said, making it sound as though he'd picked them up by mistake.

'Your pa's rich. He'll buy you more.'

Ruth crossed the room, delved into the bag and extracted a maroon velvet box. 'My necklace,' she said. 'You can't take that.'

Brent turned then. Slapped her hard across the face and took the box from her hand.

'I'll take what I want.' He turned his attention back to the safe.

Stunned by the force of his blow, Ruth ran the back of her hand over her face. When she examined it she found a smear of blood. Shocked, angry and hurting she made another grab for her jewellery box. Brent pushed her away.

'Why?' she asked. 'Why are you going?'

'Because I have to. I've got all I'm going to get here.'

'Take me with you,' she said. 'I'm your wife.'

'Why on earth would I take you? You'd be a handicap. I can travel faster without you and get another wife anywhere I go.'

'Brent!'

'I married you because it suited my purpose. Don't deceive yourself into thinking there was any other reason. I did it to antagonize Charlie Jefferson.' He hit her again, slapping both sides of her face with his right hand.

She fell to the floor. Her face felt numb, then painful. Her left eye seemed incapable of opening properly and she realized that the area below it was beginning to swell. 'I want my jewellery, Brent. Don't take my necklace and rings.'

'Shut up,' he said, fastening the bag now that he had everything of value.

'Then take me, too. Don't leave me here. I've been a good wife. I've kept the discovery of silver a secret.'

Brent stopped and glared at her. 'How long have you known about that?' She saw the fierceness in his expression, was suddenly afraid that what she had seen as a demonstration of her loyalty was clearly not how Brent saw it. 'Have you been eavesdropping? Have you?'

'It wasn't intentional. I just happened—' He hit her. Once, twice, three times, then he flung her from him. Her head hit a table leg and she lay unconscious on the floor as he made his way from the house.

The mercantile building, Sam Flint's old trading post, was his first stop. Cincinnati Enterprises provided the financial backing for all the businesses that Brent Deacon fronted in Tatanka Crossing but robbing them was a matter of no consequence to him. In a strange way he believed Cincinnati Enterprises owed him the money he was taking because, if his plan to gain the Prescott range had come to fruition, they would have had to pay him a whole lot more.

There were no living quarters attached to the store so there was no one on the premises to disturb. Furthermore, he had keys for the door and the safe so he was in and out again with the minimum of fuss and a pocketful of dollars.

The Last Dollar, his second stop, was a different matter. Not only did the girls who did business there have rooms upstairs, but Henry Wright, the barman had a cot in a small room behind the bar. That room abutted the office so if he didn't want to disturb Henry he would need to be quiet.

As it happened, Henry was up and about when Brent entered through the alley door. He'd already been disturbed by a noise from the office: someone trying to get in through the window, he thought, but when he'd investigated there had been no one there. Deacon's arrival at such a late hour had puzzled him but Brent explained that he hadn't been able to sleep so had come for some papers that required his attention. He promised Henry he would lock up on the way out, which he did while carrying a small sack containing the contents of the strongbox.

His last stop was the bank. He was grateful that Charlie Jefferson had paid off his father's loan with paper money because already the quantity of coins was too great for him to carry. He took some coins and all the paper money, which was enough to ensure he would live with a degree of affluence until the next opportunity presented itself. With three sacks of money from the bank and the carpetbag containing his collections from the other three sources, Brent Deacon directed his horse-drawn buggy slowly and quietly out of town to the west. His former home was the last building he passed.

CHAPTER FIFTEEN

That afternoon's events had been a series of disappoint-
ments for Charlie Jefferson. He'd arrived in Tatanka
Crossing with a prisoner who, Charlie was sure, could not
only clear Lars Svensson of a charge of murder but could
also provide clear evidence of Brent Deacon's involvement
in Jed Prescott's death. Although Seth Woodlow's blurted
avowal, naming Hank Swales as Jed's killer, had achieved
the first objective, his own summary murder had deprived
the town of his testimony against Deacon.

However the capture of Seth's killer would have com-
pensated for that missing testimony. Gus Tarleton was
Brent Deacon's right-hand man, therefore likely to be in
possession of more details of the banker's affairs. Having
unhorsed Tarleton, Charlie was sure he could take him
alive, but Sheriff Simms had intervened and shot him
dead. Any suspicion that the sheriff had taken that course
of action to silence Tarleton was swept from Charlie's
mind as they walked from the corral back to Main Street.

'He killed Brad Keen to avoid arrest,' Simms told
Charlie. 'He wasn't going to surrender to you or me. He
was a killer. It's my job to protect the people of the town
from men like him.'

Sheriff Simms had also made it clear to Charlie that he

had never suspected Lars of killing Jed Prescott.

'I stepped out of Doc Minchin's house that night just as the first shot was fired. Either Swales or Woodlow was thinking more quickly than I was ever likely to give them credit for when they saw me. One of them shouted out 'Lars Svensson killed Jed Prescott' and fired his gun. I saw the body on the ground and another figure climbing on a horse and did what any lawman would do. I yelled for him to stop, fired my gun in the air and hoped the boy would see sense and not become a fugitive.'

'He didn't have a gun,' Charlie had said.

'Never known the lad to carry a gun. That's why I wanted him to stop. Wanted him to prove his innocence.'

'I don't think Swales and Woodlow intended to give him the chance to do that.'

'I'm the sheriff in this town. Drifters like those two don't dictate to me.'

'But Deacon's different!'

Tom Simms had taken exception to that remark. 'Brent Deacon is an important citizen here and I treat him accordingly. That doesn't give him scope to work outside the law.'

'But you let him put up a reward for the Svensson lad.'

'I told him not to do that, but I couldn't forbid it.'

'You knew what it would lead to, such a large bounty.'

'I knew, but I couldn't forbid it, just like I couldn't forbid the little posse that was formed to catch Lars. I have no authority beyond the town limits. All I could do was include my deputy to make sure the boy wasn't lynched or killed without having the opportunity to surrender to the law.' Charlie saw sense in the sheriff's explanation even if he knew the outcome would have been different if Tarleton had ever caught Lars.

It was Simms's next words that convinced Charlie he

139

had misread the sheriff's character. 'You and I didn't get off on the right foot because I was with Brent Deacon when he came to serve notice on your father's ranch. Well, Deacon knows the law and he works inside it. He wanted me there so that your father would know that the law was on Deacon's side. I went to make it clear that the law would be upheld. That's my job.'

It was then that Charlie had had the idea of taking Tom Simms to the bank as a witness to the payment of the loan. In the back of his mind lingered the belief that the repayment of the loan might be the last straw for Brent Deacon. That this failure on top of the violence of the afternoon might coerce him into some indiscretion, might extract from him some word or action that would disclose his true purpose in Tatanka Crossing. If so, it would be an advantage to have the law present.

As it turned out, Brent Deacon's behaviour took Charlie completely by surprise; instead of dismay there was bonhomie. The anger that had consumed Charlie after his talk with Colonel MacDonald at Laramie was almost forgotten. Sheriff Simms's dictum that Brent Deacon operated within the law had lodged in his brain. The fact was that although the banker had lied to his father and Tommy Humboldt, he hadn't done anything criminal. There was no legal agreement to negotiate on their behalf, just an expectation by the ranchers that processes put in place by Sam Flint would continue under Brent Deacon. So, despite his father's high spirits because their home was safe, Charlie's mood was gloomy when they rode for home.

Dagg and Charlie parted company along the ridge, at the trail that led to the Jefferson ranch. Charlie stayed on the high ground, urging the horse into an easy run which ate up the miles to the Svensson place. His mother had wanted to get word to Taub as soon as Lars had been put to bed in the Jefferson ranch house, but Charlie had forbidden it. Until his name was cleared it was better to keep secret Lars Svensson's whereabouts. Besides, he'd promised the Svensson family he would take them news of Lars when he returned from Laramie.

When he'd told all, the Svenssons were left in a state of confusion; grateful that Lars had been cleared of Jed Prescott's murder but anxious that his wound might prove fatal.

'Thank you, Charlie, for what you have done,' said Taub. 'Who would have thought that those men who accused my son were the killers?'

'And Gus Tarleton is dead?' asked Mrs Svensson, a question she'd posed at least three times but which, yet again, brought silence to the room while she and her husband awaited Charlie's answer, as though it might be different from the previous occasions.

'He's dead.'

'He was a bad man, Charlie,' said Mrs Svensson, and she shook her head slowly as if it was impossible to believe that such a man had ever come into the Tatanka valley.

From the moment she learned of her brother's injury, Jenny had been preparing herself to ride back to the Jefferson ranch with Charlie. Charlie had warned her that Lars was weak, had lost a lot of blood, but if his system didn't become poisoned he should recover.

It was close to sundown when they got to Charlie's home and Charlie tended to the horses while Jenny went in to see her brother. He was in the grip of a fever. Mary Jefferson was applying cold cloths to his forehead and wiping his face. Jenny took over the task and stayed by his bedside all night. Watching her for a moment, Charlie

141

noted the expressions of care and concern that flashed across her face. She looked up and their eyes met. Her anxiety was clear to see; a fear that Lars wouldn't survive the night. Charlie knelt at the bed beside her, dipped a cloth in the bowl of cold water and wiped it across her brother's brow. There was little more he could do, it was merely a gesture, more for her benefit than the feverish boy's.

At that moment, Charlie had his own headache, and it concerned Brent Deacon. No matter how friendly the banker had been earlier that day, Charlie knew that the man behind that mask was still the one who had ordered Jed Prescott's murder. He had no proof of that fact, nor any idea why such an act had been necessary, but Charlie was determined he would uncover the truth.

The realization of what he had to do came to him as he watched the unconscious Lars Svensson. Lars had told him that Jed had been killed for something he'd read in Deacon's office at the back of the Last Dollar. Whatever it had been, there was no reason to suppose it wasn't still there.

'I have to go out,' he told Jenny, but he didn't go for another hour. He wanted to be sure the saloon was closed and the town asleep when he got there.

Charlie picketed the roan mare at the edge of town and made his way on foot along the back alleys to the rear of the Last Dollar. For several minutes he remained motionless in the darkness and narrowness of the gap between the saloon and the barber shop. At last, convinced that everyone within the Last Dollar was asleep, he moved to the door. Not unexpectedly, it was locked. Charlie tested the resistance of the lock and decided that trying to force it would create too much sound. He would be bound to disturb someone.

There were two windows and it was the second one he tried that enabled him to gain admittance. The frame was dry and warped, and a gap had developed near the catch. Inserting a thin blade and sliding it from left to right, he was able to disengage the fastening. He raised up the lower section and climbed through; immediately he was in the back room that Deacon used for an office.

Outside, the moon had cast enough light to make it necessary for Charlie to stick closely to the buildings to avoid any chance observation. Inside, however, it was almost total blackness and he was forced to observe a few moments of stillness to allow his eyes to become adjusted to the difference and to listen for any sound that might suggest he'd disturbed someone within the saloon.

He had never been in this room, consequently the layout of the furniture was unknown to him. He'd brought some matches but he wasn't prepared to light a lamp or even a candle to help in his search. Breaking into the saloon was a big enough risk and until there was something to examine it wasn't worth increasing the danger. He struck a match, cupped the flame with his left hand and studied the room by the brief flicker of flame.

There was a cupboard against the wall by the window. Apart from the desk in the centre of the room, this was the only piece of furniture which seemed to offer any hope of housing documents. He went to the cupboard, tried the door, tugged it, but it didn't open easily, sticking, as if the door was too big for the frame. Charlie gave a second, more forceful tug, which opened the door but also caused something inside to rattle. Charlie waited, listened for noise from within the saloon, then, when all seemed quiet, he struck another match to inspect the contents.

There was little to see: stationery items, a cash box, several books; nothing that resembled files or correspondence;

nothing that aroused Charlie's interest. In the dark he moved towards the desk, reaching it earlier than expected, kicking the leg with his tough leather riding-boot. Again he paused, waited in silence, thought he heard movement in an adjoining room, but silence settled again and he moved on.

The desk was little more than a table with a single drawer at either side. There were loose papers in the first drawer he opened. Another match showed that these were stock figures, invoices and an order book: documentation relating to the business of the Last Dollar. Charlie was sure that this was not what he wanted. In the other there was only one item; a loaded revolver. Charlie drew in a deep breath underlining his frustration at the futility of his raid. At the same moment he heard a definite movement in the adjoining room and, when the distinct glow from a lamp showed along the gap at the bottom of the door, he made his way back to the window.

As quietly as possible but with more emphasis on speed, Charlie left the building as he'd entered it, only just closing the window before the far door opened and the room was lit up by an oil lamp held high. Once outside, Charlie lost himself among the darkest recesses of the alleyways as he made his way back to the roan. At one point he thought he heard a horse and buggy close by but he didn't investigate. Disappointed by his lack of success, he climbed into the saddle and rode home.

Jenny Svensson still sat at her brother's bedside when Charlie entered the ranch house. 'How is he?' he asked, thinking Lars looked easier than when he'd gone out.

'Sleeping. I think.'

'Then you should, too,' commanded Charlie.

'I'll sit here,' she said. 'I want to be able to hear him if he calls.'

144

Charlie didn't argue with her, he knew it would be futile. 'I'm preparing some coffee. I'll bring you a cup.'

Jenny smiled. She wanted to ask him where he'd been but Lars had her full concentration and couldn't form the necessary words. When Charlie returned with the coffee she'd fallen asleep. Because it was handy, he draped his coat over her and put a cushion under her head. Then he returned to the parlour, drank his coffee and dozed while still puzzling over the problem of Brent Deacon.

The first streaks of a new day had barely touched the land when Charlie awoke with a start. He looked around, wondered if the sound that had disturbed him had come from Jenny or Lars, but it was neither. The knock was at the outer door, light, almost apologetic. Charlie opened the door and his surprise was matched by his shock.

'Ruth!'

Her face was pale and covered with bruises, cuts and dried blood. Her brow was creased with lines of pain and her eyes held an emptiness which Charlie had seen many times in men with concussion. He clutched her arms and drew her inside. 'What's happened?' Charlie thought she'd been thrown from a horse or her buggy had over-turned.

'I'm sorry, Charlie,' she said. 'I didn't know where else to go.'

Charlie led her to the seat he'd just vacated and made her sit. He went into the back, filled a bowl with water and collected a clean towel. 'What happened?' he asked as he tended to the wounds on her face.

'He's gone,' she said.

'Who? Brent?' She nodded and at the same time grimaced as Charlie dabbed and rubbed at the cut below her eye. 'Did he do this to you?'

'Yes.'

145

'Where has he gone?' Charlie couldn't keep the anger from his voice.

'Far away,' she said. 'Gone before you kill him, I guess. Or my father. Or Sheriff Simms. I know now that he was responsible for Jed's death. Sam Flint's, too.'

'He killed Sam?'

'Taking Sam Flint's role gave him a lot of power in the valley, power to unsettle everyone and make it easier for Cincinnati Enterprises to buy up the land.'

Now finished bathing Ruth's wounds, Charlie moved to clear away the dirty water. Jenny Svensson was standing in the doorway to the room where her brother lay. How long she'd been there he couldn't tell but by the way her eyes were fixed on the bowl and cloth Charlie figured it had been long enough to watch his attention to Ruth.

They were joined by Dagg and Mary Jefferson, to whom Ruth explained her husband's role on behalf of Cincinnati Enterprise and the fact that their range land was rich in mineral wealth.

'He only married me to get my father's land,' she told them. 'Knowing its true value he would sell it at a much greater price than they would expect to pay my father or anyone else in the valley.'

'But where has he gone now?' Charlie asked. 'He must be brought back to face his crimes.'

' "A city", was all he said. Somewhere he could assume another name.'

It was John, joining the group late in the explanation, who made the best suggestion. 'There are no cities within easy travelling distance,' he said, 'which means he's probably heading for the nearest railway town.'

Charlie questioned Ruth further. Had he mentioned any particular city? 'New York. New Orleans, San Francisco,' she told him, 'but that's not important. When he left town he went past our house in the buggy. That means he's heading for the northern line. Scottsbluff is the nearest railway point.'

'How much start does he have?' asked Charlie.

'Four hours. A little more.'

'Then I need to get started.'

Ruth stood, gripped Charlie's arms. 'Don't let him get away,' she implored.

Charlie told her he wouldn't, offered her something of a smile, then walked away. He slid the revolver from its holster, checked the loads and dropped it back in.

John was thinking more clearly than anyone else in the room. 'If Brent's in a buggy,' he said to Charlie, 'he'll have to stick to the trail. You can save miles going over the northern hills. With a good horse you should catch him before he reaches Scottsbluff.'

Jenny held his coat close to her, the one she had been wrapped in when she awoke. She held it out to him. She seemed subdued, as if something precious had been lost. There were so many words he wanted to say to her but all he could manage was 'Thanks.' He began to walk towards the door but she stepped in front and placed her hand on his chest. 'Take Collie,' she said. 'She's the fastest horse in the territory.'

CHAPTER SIXTEEN

Scottsbluff lay north-east of the Tatanka valley but the wagon road between them wasn't a straight line. Indeed, it was necessary to head west when leaving Tatanka Crossing, taking the route that led to the copper mine but veering north before reaching it, turning on to the long established trail into the hill country that led to the Sweetwater. Wherever possible, the route avoided those climbs and descents that were difficult for draught animals, staying instead in the low valleys, skirting the hills like a meandering stream. Consequently the journey from Tatanka Crossing to Scottsbluff was extended by many miles and although this trail was easier for wheeled vehicles it was still not suitable for travelling at great speed. In fact, by the time that Charlie Jefferson began the pursuit Brent Deacon had covered little more than thirty miles, and because of the necessary north-west loop at the start of his journey there remained little more than half that distance between them.

The sedate pace of travel was not a cause of concern for Brent Deacon. He had no reason to assume his absence would be noticed until the bank cashier tried to find him to let him know the bank had been robbed, which wouldn't be until ten o'clock, more than four hours ahead. With smug amusement he considered the antics of the townspeople when the news spread. The cashier would be running around like a headless chicken; those who had lost their money would be yelling for his capture and lynching, and Tom Simms would try to appear efficient by sending worthless telegrams to the law officers of the neighbouring towns. They would be worthless because he didn't believe Tom Simms capable of deducing Scottsbluff as his destination and, even if he did, Scottsbluff was across the border into Nebraska and the law there had no power to hold him for crimes in Tatanka Crossing. In two days he would be in St Louis, then who knew where? Dallas, Texas appealed. That was a land where a man could make his mark, and where the tendrils of Cincinnati Enterprises were unlikely to reach.

It could all have been so different, he realized, if Charlie Jefferson had not returned home. His interference alone had brought about the ruination of his schemes and, ruefully, Brent realized that he had underestimated him in every way. Charlie Jefferson had come back from the war much altered from the lad of whom he'd heard. Charlie Jefferson was resourceful and a fighter. Brent had underestimated him in many ways, not least in his marriage to Ruth. That had been done to rub salt in the wound of taking away the Jefferson ranch, but whatever effect it had had on Charlie it had not distracted him from fighting on behalf of his father or the Svensson kid. Yes, he'd underestimated Charlie Jefferson, but it was a fault he wouldn't repeat. If ever their paths crossed again he would kill him without warning.

Thoughts of Charlie Jefferson led him to consider Ruth. She, he assumed, would return to her father's ranch. Ezra Prescott would, doubtless, swear vengeance against the man who had mistreated his daughter, but he

149

had no more chance of achieving that than Sheriff Simms had of capturing him with the money. Ezra Prescott might send out riders but they would be hunting for him as aimlessly as any posse. Content with this thought, Brent Deacon drove on towards Scottsbluff.

Collie was a good three hands smaller than Smoke. She was also more barrel-bodied, making a combination which, in Charlie's experience, often meant a horse lacked speed or stamina, but this time, such an assessment never entered Charlie's mind as he threw his saddle over her back. Jenny's conviction that this was the best horse in the territory was endorsement enough. The horse had an intelligent look, her big, mainly black head turned from side to side as Charlie adjusted the saddle and reached under her belly for the cinch. Her deep brown eyes reflected her curiosity. She was accustomed to being saddled by only one person, and only that person sitting astride her back, but now that person stood silently at her head while strange hands fitted her with different harness. It was the silence that bothered Collie most. With a playful nudge she pushed Jenny with her head, needing the sound of her voice to assure her that all was well. Jenny rubbed her neck and her face as she felt the first instruction to move.

'Drop your hands to the saddle horn when you want her to run free,' Jenny told Charlie.

'Thanks, Jenny,' said Charlie. 'I'll bring Collie back safely.' With that he urged the pinto forward and out through the yard.

Jenny watched until they were little more than a distant dark smudge on the verdant landscape. 'And you bring him safely back,' she said. Her message to Collie was spoken quietly, not because she didn't want to be overheard but because the memory of Charlie's recent attention to Ruth lingered in her memory and she was afraid that when he did return it would be to the arms of another woman.

Anxious though he was to catch Brent Deacon, Charlie knew better than to set off at breakneck speed. He ran Collie, brought her down to canter then up to a gallop; he was growing accustomed to her abilities while she got to understand his instructions. It wasn't until they were at the north end of the valley, crossing Ezra Prescott's Circle P land, that he let her have her head. Harkening to Jenny's advice, he dropped his hands to the saddle horn. Feeling no pressure on the bit in her mouth, no tug on the reins, Collie ran with unbridled freedom, covering the ground with rapid strides that Charlie would have found exhilarating had his mind not been fixed on his mission to catch Brent Deacon.

In the distance, half a mile away, two Circle P cowboys watched his progress. Charlie figured they would recognize the horse if not the rider and might wonder why Jenny wasn't aboard or why it was being run with such purpose. He also wondered if Ezra Prescott had yet been informed of Lars Svensson's innocence. On reflection it seemed unlikely that none of his workers had been in Tatanka Crossing to learn of the death of Gus Tarleton, Seth Woodlow and Hank Swales.

If the cowboys recognized him they didn't give chase, but chasing would have been futile. Their working cow ponies had no more chance of catching Collie than a man had of catching a bullet from the barrel of a Winchester.

An hour after leaving his home they were in the northern hills, Charlie guiding Collie up and over hill brows and between land folds in a general north-easterly direction which would eventually bring him out on the trail to

151

Scottsbluff. The ground was firm and Collie was sure-footed. Charlie marvelled at her confidence in taking on the sudden, steep slopes, faltering little at any task. Once or twice, where surface scree added an extra challenge to a descent or climb, Charlie dropped his hands to the saddle horn and allowed Collie to pick her own route.

Eventually, from a grassy summit, Charlie saw the trail they sought. He reached forward and pulled Collie's ears the way Smoke liked his pulled.

'How far ahead is he, Collie?' Collie had no answer and for the first time a doubt entered Charlie's mind. Perhaps Brent hadn't come this way at all. Perhaps he'd deliberately left town to the west only to loop south further along the trail and was even now on a train out of Laramie. He scanned the trail ahead but there was no telltale dust signs to assure him that he hadn't miscalculated. When looking ahead offered no hope he looked along the back trail with similar result.

'Come on,' he said, tapping his heels against Collie, 'let's cover some more ground.'

They had been travelling for four hours and so far Collie had shown tremendous stamina. Varying their pace of travel helped to preserve her strength but she couldn't run for ever. From the summit Charlie had seen that the trail forded a stream about a mile ahead. He resolved to rest there for a while, which would allow Collie to cool, eat a handful of oats and drink a little stream water. Halfway to the stream he halted. Heavily laden blueberry bushes had caught his eye and as he'd only brought provisions for Collie he leapt down to gather them. Some he ate and the rest he mixed in his hat with a portion of oats for the horse. Then they walked on to the stream and that was why their approach was quiet, instead of being announced by thundering hoofbeats and rattling harness.

Brent Deacon, his back against the trunk of an old willow tree, sat in the shade. His horse and buggy were nearer the river, twenty yards off the trail where a collection of trees provided more shade for the animal. Brent was as startled to see Charlie as Charlie was to see him. For a moment neither man spoke. Then Brent laughed, a forced expression of mirth, trying to throw Charlie off guard, but his unsmiling eyes had the opposite effect. 'I didn't expect to see anyone from Tatanka Crossing along this stretch of trail.'

'I've come to take you back,' said Charlie. He drew his gun before dismounting.

'Back! Why would I want to go back?'

'It's got nothing to do with what you want. You've got to answer for the killings of Jed Prescott and Sam Flint.'

'Killings? What makes you think I had anything to do with those?'

'There's a witness. She told us about the silver and your involvement with the Cincinnati consortium that wants to buy up the valley.'

'She?'

'You shouldn't have done that to Ruth.'

'Oh. You and my wife. So that's the way it is.'

Charlie motioned with his gun. 'If you've got a gun under that jacket you'd better throw it on the ground now.'

Deacon shook his head. 'No gun.' He spread his jacket to prove the fact.

'What about your pockets?'

'I'm not armed,' Deacon said, patting at his sides to show that the pockets were empty.

Charlie motioned him towards the buggy. 'Let's check that,' he said, 'then we'll start back.' As they approached, Charlie could see the sacks and carpetbag on the floor.

153

'What's in those?'

'Money,' admitted Brent, realizing that Charlie must have left Tatanka Crossing before the robbery had been reported. 'I'll share it with you. All you have to do is let me continue on my way. You'll never hear from me again. You can have Ruth, too.'

For that moment, Charlie's attention had been mainly centred on the bags in the buggy but Brent Deacon's words riled him and he looked up just as the banker pulled the whip from its holder on the buggy and lashed out. The knotted cord struck Charlie across the chest and before he could gather his senses he was lashed again. This time the strike cut across the hand that held the gun and it fell to the ground. Deacon tried again with the whip but it was nothing more than a token swing across the buggy, intended to keep Charlie off balance rather than do any actual harm. The reason was that Deacon had a revolver on the seat, tucked tight against the side. He fired, but Charlie, in attempting to avoid the whip lash, stumbled and fell and the shot went wide.

Once again Deacon raised his pistol but with Charlie on the ground and the buggy between them he couldn't get a clear shot. Charlie looked around for his own gun but couldn't see it. Deacon was moving now, intending to come around the front of the horse to finish off Charlie. Charlie's hand settled on a small rock. Instantly he threw it at the horse's rump. As a result of the unexpected strike, it jerked forward and knocked Deacon to the ground. With a curse he fired again at Charlie. It was a hurried shot that kicked up dust to Charlie's left but it also had another unsettling effect on his horse. It moved forward, its eyes rolling, ready to bolt if spooked again.

Charlie saw his revolver. It was beneath the buggy and inaccessible. Thinking quickly and taking advantage of

Deacon's inability to get off a clear shot, Charlie set off in a stooped run to cover the six or seven yards to Collie. Just as a shot rang out he dived forward and went under Collie's belly. As he got to his feet he pulled his Winchester from its scabbard and at the same time slapped Collie on the rump to move her away from the line of fire. He dived forward. By this time Brent Deacon had moved clear of his buggy and was advancing with gun in hand. When Collie moved he fired but Charlie was full length on the ground to the left of where Deacon expected him to be. Charlie fired three times. Each bullet struck Deacon's chest and he was dead when he hit the ground.

CHAPTER SEVENTEEN

The following Sunday their friends from Tatanka Crossing and all along the valley were invited to the Jefferson ranch. Ostensibly, the gathering was to welcome Charlie home but the people came also to honour his recent achievements. Within a week of his return to the Tatanka valley his actions had cleared the town of gunfighters, proved the innocence of a young man accused of murder and returned the money that had been stolen from their bank.

While, on the surface, these things seemed to be a matter of restoring peace and order to the Tatanka valley, everyone knew that it would never be the same again. Civilization was spreading west and the revelation of the mineral deposits would inevitably force changes. Perhaps, when a true value was assessed, Tommy Humboldt, Ezra Prescott, Taub Svensson and even Dagg Jefferson might be tempted into selling the mineral rights. They might even sell the land itself. It would be each man's choice. However, they were united in their determination that no man would sell any part of the valley to Cincinnati Enterprises.

Mary Jefferson had been preparing for the event for the

best part of a week and was pleased to have been rewarded with a warm, bright day. The Kincaid family had arrived early that morning, their flat wagon bearing not only mother, father and daughter Lucy, but also pies, savouries and sweet things that were the usual fare of their eating house. At the side of the house, tables were set up, draped with cloths and loaded with foodstuffs. John Jefferson, who had seldom been near a table any longer than was necessary to eat a meal, was all fingers and thumbs over domestic work as he tried to assist Lucy Kincaid. His bashful need to stay by her side was as much a source of quiet pleasure to the two mothers as his clumsy handling of food-covered plates was a cause of their annoyance. There was barely a piecrust unbroken by his thumb.

The visitors arrived during the course of the morning, among them Ezra Prescott with his son Zach and daughter, Ruth. Dagg and Mary had sent an invitation to the Circle P but weren't sure that the Prescotts would turn up; however they were the first to greet them when they drove through the gate.

'Good to see you, Ezra,' Dagg said as he held out his hand. It was clear from the smile and firm grasp that the greeting was genuine. Mary enquired after Zach's injury, his arm was still in a sling for protection. She greeted Ruth warmly but had still not forgiven the girl for her behaviour the night Charlie was dining at the Svensson ranch.

'Spying,' she had told her husband when Ruth had gone. 'Spying and they mean to harm Charlie.'

But now Brent Deacon was dead and Mary Jefferson was unsure what that meant to her son. He'd returned home expecting Ruth Prescott to be waiting for him. Perhaps, now, Charlie would renew his hopes for her. Mary hoped not, but there was no way of predicting people's reactions in such circumstances.

157

Charlie had spoken to Doc Minchin and his family, Tom Simms and Tommy Humboldt while wandering around the yard. He'd stayed close to the corral which had been set aside for the visitors' horses, watching the arrivals, ready with a word for everyone. Ezra Prescott approached him without bombast. 'There are things we should discuss,' he said.

Charlie tipped his head slightly, unsure what was on Ezra Prescott's mind. 'Mr Prescott, the last time we spoke I told you I had no argument with you. That still applies. Let's just shake hands and be friends.'

'There's the business of the cattle sold to the military. I didn't know that Brent had only used my stock to fill the contract. I wasn't trying to bring about the ruin of Tommy Humboldt or your father.'

'I don't think either of them thought that, but it would be a simple matter to make amends. Buy five hundred head from each of them. That should keep them afloat until this business with the minerals is sorted.'

As Ezra nodded his agreement, Charlie saw the Svensson family approaching the gate. Taub and his wife sat up front with Lars in the back of the buggy. After his fever had broken, the lad was soon on the mend. He'd returned home the day after Charlie killed Brent Deacon and now, although still pale, he looked happy despite the fact that dismounting from the carriage caused him a deal of discomfort.

Jenny was astride Collie. Charlie saw her looking in his direction but there was no indication of pleasure in what she saw. A voice at his side distracted him. 'I never did thank you properly, Charlie, for tending to my injuries,' Ruth Deacon said.

Charlie inspected her face. Most of the cuts had healed and the swellings had disappeared. The discolorations that remained had been covered over with feminine paint and powder. She wore a green dress, no hint of black or any sign of mourning for her dead husband. 'None needed,' he answered, 'I'd've done as much for anyone.'

'Perhaps some day, Charlie,' Ezra Prescott said, 'we'll talk about Amos over a glass of whiskey.'

'I'd like that, Mr Prescott,' Charlie said, 'but for now you must excuse me. There's something I need to do.'

Charlie went to the stable. When he emerged a few minutes later he was riding Smoke. The grey was well rested, stepping high and looking eager to run. Charlie steered his horse towards the yard gate where Jenny stood, talking to his mother.

'Where are you going?' his mother asked, astonished that he was leaving the gathering.

'I've got to get away for a while,' he told her. 'All these people talking like I'm some kind of hero, it's embarrassing. Besides, Smoke needs a good run.'

'Are you going alone?'

Jenny turned away, looked across the yard as though expecting another rider to emerge from the stable. But Ruth Deacon, somewhat forlorn, stood beside her father.

'I sure am,' Charlie answered his mother, 'unless somebody with a pot-bellied pinto has other ideas.'

'Pot-bellied pint. . . .' Jenny Svensson's outrage died immediately when she saw Charlie's grin.

'Think you can beat me to the white rock?' he asked, then with a wild yell, he set Smoke to a gallop across the grass land.

'Hey!' Jenny shouted, aggrieved that he'd taken a head start but flushed with happiness that he'd chosen to meet her at Bull Creek, her favourite spot in the valley. In an instant she gathered up Collie's reins and mounted her on the run, like a pony express rider at a change-over station.

159

She didn't yell like Charlie, she put all her concentration into catching up to the horse and rider ahead. Despite all her past claims, the prime reason wasn't to prove that Collie was the better horse.

Dagg Jefferson joined his wife and indicated his eldest son's shy attention to Lucy Kincaid. 'Perhaps if we hire that girl as our new cook he'll get the message that we don't mind having her around the place.' Mary smiled at her husband's assumed testiness. She'd spoken to Lucy and knew John's days as a single man were numbered. 'On the other hand,' added Dagg who now gazed across to the far mound where Charlie had halted to wait for Jenny, 'it seems that the best horse doctor in the valley is going to join the family after all.'